Subversion

A Tayt Waters Mystery

Book One

J.P. Choquette

Other books by J.P. Choquette

Epidemic

Dark Circle

Subversion. Copyright © 2014 by J.P. Choquette. All rights reserved. Printed in the United States of America.

Library of Congress Cataloging-in-Publication Data

Subversion / Choquette, J.P.--1st CreateSpace Paperback ed.
Copyright © 2014 J.P. Choquette

ISBN-10: 1500963402

ISBN-13: 978-1500963408

DEDICATION

To my sisters, Céleste, Faith and Aimee, who consistently teach me what it means to be a strong woman.

ACKNOWLEDGMENTS

The great thing about being a reader during the acknowledgements section (unlike, say, a member of the audience at the Emmy's), is that you can skip right over the "thank yous." But these will be short and sweet, promise.

Many thanks to my critique partners, Cori Lynn Arnold and Mary Sutton, fellow authors and Sisters in Crime members. Your suggestions and great insights have made the book better. Thanks also to Pat Gratton, Angela Lavery, Brian Noyes and Lucinda Miller for your review of an early manuscript and excellent discernments.

Aimee Perrino, my editor extraordinaire--thank you for your great catches and patience with my "comma issues." And many thanks to Malcolm Hamblett, who spent countless hours proofreading. I take full responsibility for any leftover typos.

I also would like to thank Susan Randall of Vermont Private Eye for the time and energy you gave to this project.

Finally, I thank YOU the reader (if you've gotten this far!). Without you, writing books wouldn't be nearly as much fun. Thanks for continuing to support my work.

Lastly, to Serge, for sticking by me on this sometimes rocky road of book creation. Your support means everything.

~Dios Amore~

CHAPTER ONE

It's taken me twenty-nine years to realize this fact: People are pigs.

I'm on my hands and knees scrubbing the crap out of a section of mulberry colored carpet in a second floor bathroom. The crap, I should clarify, is the literal kind. Dried on like cement. It's been there awhile. Dumping the remains of a bottle of piney smelling industrial cleaner on it, I leave the liquid to do its thing.

My name is Tayt Waters. I'm nearing the three decade mark, and in case you wondered, no, this is not my dream job. I opened my cleaning business: "Repo Renew," five years ago at the ripe old age of twenty-four. The business name sort of says it all, but I did add this catchy little tagline to my business cards, "We make it look brand new!" In a nutshell, my job is to clean houses that have been foreclosed on. I take on other cleaning jobs, too, when I'm in need of extra cash. Which is just about always.

But that's just my first job. Two years ago I opened my own security firm, T.R. Waters Security, housed in a derelict building in downtown St. Albans. Here I act as skip tracer locating missing persons, from dead beat dads to lost loves from years past. I also do general grunt work for nearly any situation requiring extra security.

I glance at my watch, nearly one o'clock. My stomach whines, reminding me that I haven't had lunch yet. I debate for a minute then check the carpet in the bathroom again. The heavy duty cleaner has done its thing. I begin alternately rinsing and patting the area dry but am interrupted by my ringing cell phone. I pull it out of my bag, but the screen is blank, the phone silent. I hear the ringing again and realize it's coming from the second phone I keep, this one a cheap pay-as-you-go type.

"Hello," I say.

A woman's voice, dry and brittle like old tree roots, responds. My mind immediately creates an image: mid-fifties, brown hair turning gray, wrinkled face with a downturned mouth and an angry pull to the eyebrows.

"I need some help with my husband, Walter. A friend," she pauses for a moment, "a friend told me about your Sunflower Specials."

"Great," I say and scramble for paper and a pen. Calls answered at this number require discretion, and this woman has said the magic phrase, "Sunflower Specials." We make arrangements to meet at a small coffee shop on Main Street later this afternoon.

"I'm a redhead," I say, "and I'll be wearing all black."

The air is chilly outside, dry leaves blowing around my feet as I pull the heavy door closed and double check the lock. The sky overhead is robin's egg blue without a single cloud. This will change shortly. Vermont in late autumn, a good part of winter and most of spring, is covered in thick, gray clouds. In other words, for about seven months of the year, it's dreary, cold and pitiful looking. This is something that rarely ends up on postcards, however, leaving tourists filled with shock and dismay that every day in the Green Mountain State isn't, in fact, made up of a Norman Rockwell'esque landscape.

The door on my rusted Toyota squeals like a squirrel who's just been informed he has a nut allergy. I ignore the racket; it will soon be drowned out by the angry growl of a muffler sporting yet another hole. Out of habit, my eyes travel to the inspection sticker planted beneath the rearview mirror.

"We've got two more months, baby," I croon to the hulking beast as I back him out of the driveway. "You've gotta get yourself together." My sedan seems to snort in response, a puff of dreary smoke coughing from the tailpipe. I ignore this response and turn on the radio. Loud African tribal music drowns out the rest of the car's protests.

I follow the winding back road onto Route 7, the main artery that runs nearly the length of the state. The scenery outside the windows is the same as it's been for the last few weeks: brilliant gold and fiery red leaves mixed with an orange so bright it nearly glows. I turn up the heat but crack the window, breathing in the scent of pine and earth and the slightly sweet smell of decaying leaves. And of course, exhaust fumes.

Stopping by the gas station across from the Highgate Shopping Plaza, I pick up lunch: a tuna sandwich on wheat, chips and a flavored seltzer. I eye the jumbo sized chocolate chip cookies and end up nabbing one at the last minute. A nagging voice in my

5

head reminds me that I missed my visit at the gym yesterday.

I'll go later.

Really.

I sip and crunch and chew my way through lunch watching businesses, then residential lots pass my windows. I make a right onto Lower Newton and then a left on Federal Street, passing a milk creamery and farm store along with more houses, these on postage sized lots, some with chipped paint and crumbling foundations. Stowing the lunch wrappers in the garbage bag, I wipe my hands on a napkin and brush crumbs from my jeans. I'll change in the office where I keep a few extra changes of professional-looking clothes and a toothbrush.

I make a right onto Lake Street and look for a parking spot near a string of tired buildings after crossing the railroad tracks. As usual there is none. I turn into the parking lot and find a sunny place for the sedan.

Living or working "below the tracks" is a derogatory comment here in Rail City, but I'm just grateful for an honest to goodness office, however humble. Sure, it's located in a sketchy part of town. All of the buildings on this street have seen better days. If they could express feelings, they'd wag fingers and shake disapproving heads at the newly remodeled Main Street.

Neglected or not, I always feel a little thrum of excitement as I mount the stairs to the second floor. It's an adventurous climb; one never knows what might be found on the steps. I've discovered everything from a pair of rats, to a creepy-looking baby doll, to a drunk

6

guy and once, an orange cat the size of a small car. The latter clattered down so fast and unexpectedly I nearly had a heart attack.

Today, however, the steps are bare. They creak, and one or two wobble under my weight. I unlock and open the goldenrod door. A smile spreads over my face as I look for the eightieth time at the lettering professionally rendered on the door in white: *T. R. Waters' Security.*

Choosing a title was hard. I'd considered at one time becoming a full-on PI, working with state and federal agencies, but then I came to my senses. I want action without the red tape. As a security expert, I can throw a wider net, picking up jobs that aren't law-enforcement related. Sometimes a bar needs extra security for a weekend event, or a traveling musician requires additional help for a concert and sometimes my job is to use my sleuthy skills to spy and track someone down. Not uninteresting work and definitely better than sitting in government meetings for hours on end.

I clean up in the tiny bathroom that's barely big enough to turn around in. A miniature dresser in one corner holds extra clothes. I change and brush my teeth, then my hair, pinning it up in a loose bun. It's medium brown and exactly matches my eyes. Eyes, teeth and nose are all straight, a good thing I guess. I'm no beauty queen like my mother and older sister. A smattering of freckles across my nose and cheeks makes me look younger than I am. I smooth the polyester button down (no hanging required) over my waist. My figure is one I'm proud of. I'm petite but muscular. All that time in the gym and my mixed martial arts classes paid off at last. I stuff my clothes from this morning's housecleaning into a grocery bag to bring home and launder.

My office is made up of a single room of about fifteen by twenty. File cabinets, mostly empty, hunker along one wall. Another wall displays a bulletin board where I've tacked up newspaper articles of interest along with a copy of my brochure, business card and a list of professional references. The third wall holds a small set of built-in bookcases and a conference table sits in front of it. The last wall is divided by two large, nearly floor-to-ceiling windows. Though drafty in the winter, I wouldn't trade them for anything. Natural light pours into the room which would otherwise have a closet-like feel. Between the windows is my desk, a vintage, army green metal beast that I bought at a surplus sale. A coffee pot along with fixings and a few clean mugs and spoons perch on a small credenza that I found outside the local Salvation Army, so ugly even they didn't want it. But a fresh coat of paint and a new leg have rejuvenated it.

I've barely started checking email when a knock sounds at my door. Must be my one o'clock appointment. I stand, smooth my shirt and put on a smile. Again the tentative knock sounds, then a hand snakes around the frame of the door pushing it open.

"Hello?" The voice is male.

I start moving toward the door then stop in my tracks. My breath catches so tightly in my throat that I nearly choke on it. Directly in front of me with a face as familiar as my own stands a man who makes me wish I were a hundred miles away. Or even two.

Just not here.

SUBVERSION

Anywhere but here.

CHAPTER TWO

"Tatum Rose, I'm so glad to see you," Jack Waters says. He stands just under six feet, tall and lanky, hair in need of a trim, lines crisscrossing his face like rail yard tracks. He looks older than the last time I saw him, tired and worn down but still just as handsome. His clothes, expensive as always, are wrinkled. A coating of dust covers his normally sparkling wing tips.

"Sorry to barge in like this, unexpected," he goes on. My feet have turned to roots dug deep into the ugly carpet. I can't locate my voice, but my heartbeat hammering in my chest tells me that this isn't a dream.

"I didn't know where else to go." Jack's voice breaks then, and he looks out the large windows, rubbing his left hand over his face wearily.

"May I?" He flaps the same hand toward one of the two chairs facing my desk. I nod, mutely, then turn and nearly fall into my office chair. The barrier of the green beast between us feels good.

"What are you doing here?" I ask, my voice low and surprisingly steady. I force my face into a poker stance, pray that he can't see my heartbeat through my shirt.

"Aren't you going to offer your old man some coffee?"

I shake my head.

"Can't. Sorry. I have an appointment in a few minutes." My voice sounds anything but sorry. "Why don't you tell me why you're here?" I repeat the last words slowly, but my mind is spinning. A thousand images of our past play out before me like a jerky movie reel: Jack tossing me high into the air, my long hair streaming as I squeal in delight, playing tickle monster and hide and seek and endless games of Monopoly. And then the later years: the lines appearing on his face after long days traveling for work; the endless phone calls about mergers and outsourcing and bottom lines; the late nights; the fights between him and my mother and the hot, strangling anger which became an additional member of our family.

I clear my throat, waiting.

He's looking out the windows again, then gets up to pace in front of them.

"I'm in some trouble, Tatum; I think it's pretty bad. I thought because you're a PI and all, you might ..."

I hold up a hand, "Whoa, wait a minute. I'm not a private investigator." I point to the door and the lettering. "I do missing person searches and general security work—you know, as a guard or bouncer at a concert—that type of thing. Between that and Repo Renew, I have my hands full." I clear my throat which is slowly loosening enough for me to breathe normally.

"I can give you Judy Palmer's card, though. Did you ever meet her? She's been my informal mentor for years, and she's one of the best investigators in the state." I'm babbling, but my father isn't filling in any of the awkward pauses. I run a finger through my Rolodex

11

(yup, I'm old-school) and find a few of Judy's cards. I push one across the desk to Jack, who is still staring at a spot over my head. Then he looks at his shoes and moves one against the other as though trying to remove the layer of dirt. Finally, he glances at me. His eyes are sad, but I recognize another emotion there. One that no child wants to see in their parent's face: fear.

"What happened, Jack?" My words are soft. I still hate him, but a small part of my chest is loosening like thread coming out of a knot.

He sighs then rubs both hands over his face, scrubbing.

"I don't want to mess up your appointments. I know how hard it is when you work for yourself, and you're just starting out. Listen, Tatum, would you meet me later for a coffee? Not in town, though," he adds before I can answer. "I'll pick you up when you're done here."

Pause. Long and uncomfortable. I fumble with my date book. The late afternoon slots are wide open.

"I guess."

He smiles then, a sad smile that doesn't reach his eyes.

"What time?"

I check my appointment book again.

"Four-thirty would be OK."

"Four-thirty it is. You parked in the lot?"

I nod.

"I'll pick you up there. I drive a silver BMW." He didn't need to tell me this. My father has been driving variations of silver BMWs my whole life.

"Fine. I'll see you then." I stand, move toward the door. He takes my hint and walks out in front of me. Just before I close the door behind him, he pauses, puts a hand out to stop the door.

"Thanks," he says. I nod once and close the door as soon as he's withdrawn his hand.

I listen to his footsteps on the creaking wood stairs, praying that they won't give out and at the same time wishing he'd break his neck.

What is he doing here? And how long has it actually been since I've seen him? I walk to the window with a partial street view but can't see his retreating figure. Two years, maybe three. We've kept in touch sporadically via phone. Well, OK. Mostly a few voicemails he's left which I haven't returned. I know he keeps in touch with Mama which is likely how he found my office. I can't believe she still speaks to him.

My one o'clock appointment is a no-show. I spend the next hour shuffling paperwork and responding to email. T.R. Waters Security's website traffic has picked up, Google Analytics informs me, which is good news. It's probably due to the recent ad in the paper. I water the plants and plump the pillows and make my mind go blank whenever my father's face appears in it. It's an old trick that's served me well over the years.

Movement catches my eye as I stare out the window and I glance at the big white house across the street. It's pretty, or used to be. A large Victorian, it has all the original gingerbread trim and a wide front porch, but peeling paint and sagging stairs take away from the charm. Alinah is out on the front porch shaking out a rug. I grab my jacket and pick my way down the stairs carefully then jog across the street.

"Good afternoon!" I call out.

Her dark head rises, a smile on her beautiful brown face.

"Afternoon," she says, her voice heavily accented.

The air is chilly, our breath making little steamy orbs that dissipate seconds later. Alinah is wearing a thin cotton blouse and a pair of jeans. Her feet are bare.

"Aren't you cold?"

She nods, smiling. Her hands continue shaking the rug, and I notice a broom nearby.

"Can I help?"

"Oh no. No, no, thank you."

Alinah is the most beautiful woman I've ever seen in real life. Her body is slender, hair dark and thick, face wide with perfectly formed cheekbones. Her eyes are almond-shaped and lined with thick black lashes. I would hate her if I didn't like her so much.

"Want to come up for coffee?" I ask her this time and again, but she's only joined me once, and even then, seemed uncomfortable.

"Oh, no. Thank you, but I have much work to do."

Her hands are trembling, and when I look more closely I notice her eyes are pink-rimmed.

"Is everything OK?"

Her hands stop moving the rug. She glances at me, then away, then at the floor of the porch.

"Sarjana, my cousin? She missing." Her voice is so low that I strain to hear.

"Missing?" I keep my voice quiet, but Alinah puts a finger over her lips, shushing me.

"I no can talk now. Maybe later you come back." She smiles at me, but it doesn't reach her eyes. Then she moves back into the house, waves and closes the door behind her.

I gnaw on a hangnail as I cross back over to my office building. Sarjana is younger than Alinah, a cousin from Malaysia, I think. The two moved here from New York City several months ago but they stick to themselves. They share the house with a white guy, Sarjana's boyfriend, Doug, Alinah told me. He's got a lot of tattoos and a nearly shiny bald head, and he looks at me in a way that makes my skin crawl.

CHAPTER THREE

It's just after two o'clock when I arrive back at my office. I unlock it and spend the next fifteen minutes applying makeup, a red, bobbed wig, a pair of fake reading glasses and a black business suit. I switch out my regular canvas messenger bag for a sleek leather briefcase, add a notepad with extra pens. I call for a cab and wait two blocks from my office building just in case the taxi driver has an excellent memory. Five minutes later he deposits me at a small coffee shop at the southern end of Main Street. I could have walked, but the stiletto heels make the process rather uncomfortable.

Mary Ann Hawk is tiny and bird-like and does have the dark hair and wrinkles I expected but not the angry eyebrows. Instead, her eyebrows are nearly invisible, almost plucked to extinction. I order coffees for both of us, and we sit at a table with a view of the street.

"I got me a problem with my husband, Walter. I told you that on the phone," she says. "He's a maniac. A crazy man. And when he gets to drinkin' ..." she leaves the sentence unfinished, staring intently at the large windows as though her estranged husband is watching from the street. And what do I know? He could very well be.

"So, Mrs. Hawk. Mary Ann. Is it OK to call you

that?"

She nods, twisting the thin curtain between clenched fingertips.

"Your husband, Mr. Walter Hawk, has a history of abusing you."

"Yeah. If you can call nearly killin' me abuse, then yeah. I almost died that last time," she laughs, a deep, dry sound. "He messed me up so good that it took me weeks to recover. Thought I might not for a while there, but here I am."

Her fingers strangle the paper napkin. I nod, make a note on my paper.

"How's all this work, anyway?" she asks, looking at me. "My friend said that you take on these special jobs, Sunflower Specials she called 'em. Said you can track people down, make 'em pay for what they done."

I nod, hoping my wig stays in place.

"Are you familiar with Iranian law?" I ask.

Mary Ann nods, then shrugs. "Not really. I guess not."

"In Iran it's called Capital Punishment. The law states that the victim of a crime, or the victim's family, if the victim is deceased, is responsible for exacting punishment on the criminal. Not on their own, but as part of a legal process."

Mary Ann's eyes brighten.

I continue, "Say for instance that a man is killed in a street fight. After a legal trial where the perpetrator is convicted, the victim's family will be the ones at the hanging, responsible for pushing the chair out from under the murderer."

"Pffft," Mary Ann says, squinting her eyes at me.

"So you're sayin' you'll bring, what, bring Walter to me? No offense, but that ain't gonna do me an ounce of good. You don't think if I could give him what he's got coming, I'd have done it before now?" Mary Ann pauses for her first sip of coffee. Her skinny arm shakes slightly.

"That's where I come in," I say, lowering my voice further. "Think of me as your sort of rented family. I'll see that Walter is punished. My job in these cases," I'm whispering now and Mary Ann leans closer to me, so close that I can see every pore in her nose, "is to make sure that the punishment fits the crime."

"And then you just go along your merry little way?" she says. Her breath smells like coffee and spearmint.

"I do have two rules in regards to Sunflower Specials," I say, tapping the table with a nail to enunciate each. "The first is that the perpetrator actually is a perpetrator. I'm not going to go around scooping up innocent people for psychopaths," I take a sip of my drink. "No offense."

"None taken. I can get you court papers, photos of me from the hospital if that's what you want."

"That is exactly what I'm looking for," I say, leaning back in my chair and returning my voice to a normal volume. "Once you give me those and your retainer, we can move on with your case."

"You said you had two rules. So, what's the second?"

"I get paid in cash, half up front and half when I deliver. No checks, no credit cards, no IOUs."

"How much is a job like this gonna set me back?" Mary Ann asks, taking another sip of her coffee. I tell her, and she chews her lip a while, then nods.

"I can get it to you by the end of this week."

"That would be fine. Call me again when you have the money and the documents, and I'll get started. In the meantime, why don't you tell me a little bit about Walter: where he likes to hang out, where he works, what his hobbies are. Did you bring a photo?"

Walter Clement Hawk, born June 30, 1956, has been on disability for the past twelve years. He spends most of that, along with a meager pension from his previous factory career, on booze, guns—which he uses to hunt illegally, according to Mary Ann—and cards. His favorite place to hang out is a scuzzy bar just a few blocks away.

"Where have you been living since ..." My voice peters out momentarily, "since that last time?"

"My car." The tiny woman reaches into her jacket pocket and extracts a crumpled fist of tissues, blows her nose. She sounds like a Canadian goose. An older businessman at the table nearby glances our way.

"You can't stay in your car, Mary Ann. It's not safe."

"Well, where am I supposed to go?" She spits the words out like pins, sharp and hard. "I can't go home. If I stay in my car I can keep moving around. If I go home, he'll be there, or if he's not staying there he'll find me for sure. I can't take that chance."

"What about the women's crisis center?"

Mary Ann snorts. "I'm not holing up in there with a bunch of ninnies. He'll find me, and then what? They got cops on duty 24/7?"

I shake my head.

"I don't think so. But the location is secure, and I know that the police monitor it."

"Nah. No, thanks. I'll take my chances on my own. I got my car and some cash. You do your job and I'll be OK."

The hardness of her voice melts a little around the edges.

"You really think you'll find him?" she asks.

I nod.

"He's a mean man."

"Well, I'm tougher than I look," I say.

She nods in response, staring at her ball of tissues.

"I don't know how much longer I can do this," she mumbles so low that I can hardly hear. "I still love him, you know." She snorts a laugh at this, wipes hard-looking hands roughly over her eyes. "I know that makes me stupid in your eyes, but it's the truth. Anyway," she sighs hard, whooshing out air from her lungs, "it don't matter. He's never gonna change, and I can't take living with him no more. After what he did to me that last time ..." Her voice drifts off momentarily.

"You find him and take care of him. Make sure he don't wanna come near me again. You do that and I'll be OK." Straightening her shoulders she dries angry eyes and stares out the large windows.

CHAPTER FOUR

Back at my office, I change clothes again, wash my face and box up the wig. The parking lot is nearly empty when I emerge just after four-thirty. The glare from the descending sun illuminates my car and a broken down Hyundai on blocks. No silver BMW.

I balance my bag against my hip while pocketing the key to my office, looking around the area with a practiced gaze. Awareness, not diamonds, is a girl's real best friend. I remember a statistic from one of my first martial arts classes: More than half of all attacks are preventable if a woman is just aware of her surroundings.

In this situation I see what I do every evening: rundown buildings surrounding a parking lot that's in serious need of repaving. The asphalt buckles and pops where frost heaves and overly aggressive snow plows have ravaged it. The city has sent road crews more than once in recent years to repair the damage. Black strips of tar and spots here and there, where new, black asphalt has been laid, make the remainder of the lot look only more run-down.

I cross to the rusty car, shove my bag into the back seat and climb in behind the wheel to wait for my father. The air is chilly and wet feeling, dampness rising up from the pavement and shimmying in around the edges of the car's doors and windows. I turn the engine over and crank up the heat dial only to be rewarded with a blast of frigid air.

"Come on, baby," I say, patting the dashboard. "Give Mama some heat." The Toyota, all male, sits stubbornly and continues to puff coldness out of the vents. I finally give up and turn the dial back down. Shivering, I clap my hands together to warm them then remember my spare jacket under the passenger seat and retrieve it.

As I wait, my thoughts return to Walter and what my best plan of attack is. The bar he hangs out in most frequently is just off of Catherine Street, a place called, "The Trap." Not sure who is in charge of their marketing, but they should probably be fired. Rat trap, fire trap and death trap spring immediately to mind. I've been to the place only once, looking for a runaway teenaged girl over a year ago.

An idea for Walter has been percolating since I left the café. The second Thursday of each month a lowlife in Fairfield plays host to blood thirsty crowds in pit fights on his ramshackle farm. So far these have remained off the radar of the state police. Or maybe they're too busy with DUIs and domestic abuse situations to care about grown men and women bloodying their neighbors' faces for a little cash.

Pulling my checkbook from my bag, I squint at the tiny calendar on the back. It takes a few seconds to figure out which day of the month this is. Things have been so busy that they've all mixed together. This Thursday is fight night, just two days away. I feel a tremor of both excitement and fear wiggling in my chest.

Blowing on my hands, I cup them around my mouth, savoring the warm air. My fingertips are numb, and I'm wishing I had moved the cold-weather emergency box into the trunk.

"Come on, come on," I mutter. The car must finally be feeling sympathetic because when I try the heat dial this time, warm air blasts from the vents.

Where is Jack? I glance at the dimly lit clock on the dash. It's nearly five. I sigh, roll my shoulders. Ten more minutes. Mary Ann seems motivated and assured me she could get both the documentation of her abuse and the money by tomorrow. If I'm able to nab Walter at The Trap the same night as the pit fight, everything might work out perfectly. I smile.

I'm debating the best time to try to find Walter at the bar when I see Doug leaving the white house across the street. He pulls out a cell phone, has a brief conversation and looks back at the big house before retreating to the backyard.

Has Sarjana returned? Maybe it was a late night somewhere, and she decided to sleep over rather than drive back to St. Albans. But then the girls don't have a car, do they? I try to remember if I've ever seen either of them behind the wheel. I don't think so.

Memories of my father crowd in despite my best attempts to reroute them elsewhere. Whereas before, the memories came in short, snapshot rapid fire, now the memories are slower, languid. I remember the conversation we had shortly before he left home that last time, the way he looked: pained and sad. I didn't know what was coming before that conversation, but I think

Mama did. Sophie, too. I guess it was just me and Max who were too naïve, too blind to see it coming. I remember the impromptu game of baseball he played with Max and me, the hotdogs and popcorn afterward and that last trip together to the lake for a picnic lunch. After years of distance and busyness I should have suspected that Jack was, in his own way, saying goodbye.

It had hit Max hardest. He'd always been like a miniature version of my father. Or at least, he'd tried to be. He wanted so hard to please the man, always waiting to show him his report card before letting our mother see it, always following on my father's heels, asking him to play a board game or toss his baseball around. My father's response was typically, "Not now, Max," but occasionally he would agree. Max's face would light up like a thousand candles, and he'd grab Dad's hand as though, if he weren't physically holding onto him his father might disappear, vaporize.

Like he did tonight, apparently.

When I get home, there is a cow blocking my driveway. This is not an uncommon occurrence in the country, unfortunately. I honk the horn, and the black and white splotched Holstein looks at me as if to say, "Excuse me? Can't you see I'm eating here?" And she is, happily munching away on what's left of my flower garden.

"For pity's sake." I throw off my seatbelt and eject myself from the car, door squealing. That sound, for whatever reason, gets the cow's attention. She looks uneasily now from me to the car and back again.

"Go home!" I yell, waving my arms.

Munch, munch, munch.

"Are you serious? It's been a long day, Daisy or Buttercup, or whatever your name is. I'm tired and cold and looking forward to putting my feet up and enjoying a glass of wine. So scram."

The cow juts her big head forward and utters a low *moooooo.*

I throw up my hands. Grabbing my bag from the car, I retreat to my trailer.

I bought the mobile home and land two years ago when I first decided that my dreams of making it to New York City or Los Angeles to pursue a career in acting were over. I'd rented before that, two different but equally tidy and small apartments close to St. Albans, but I never felt completely comfortable in either. I guess it's a good thing that I never had the chance to try city living. Even the close quarters of town gave me the heebie-jeebies. I didn't like looking out my window and seeing the neighbor in his bathrobe or the dog next door peeing on my potted tomato plants on the front stoop. That nearly cured me of gardening completely.

Here, I live in a trailer, yes, but it's mine. And it's not bad looking. I've modified it, adding a covered porch on the front and a small sunroom and deck off the back for more hours and square feet of growing time in my mini greenhouse. In the summer, I have a big garden. I've yet to do the full homestead thing and raise flocks of chickens or ducks, but if this cow sticks around long enough she might end up as steaks in the freezer.

Stepping through the door, my shoulders lower. It smells good. A mix of leftover coffee, lavender and traces of breakfast toast. I drop my bag on a chair near the door, pull off my boots and wiggle my toes while flipping through the mail. Bills, more bills and two sale flyers.

The last of the afternoon sunlight is bouncing off the windowpanes, eking weak rays into the small room, when a knock sounds at the door. I haul myself out of the cushy chair I'd been snoozing in and grumble my way to the door. The peephole reveals my neighbor Winston's balding head, a crazy scraggle of gray hair poking up around the outer rim.

"Hey," I say, opening the door.

Winston looks from the cow to me, startled.

"That your cow?" His voice is gruff. He's wearing a pair of old canvas green pants tied with a length of stained rope, a flannel shirt with a jagged tear down the left arm. The buttons are fastened crookedly. A dirty white t-shirt peeks out of the checkered shirt.

"No," I say, motioning for him to come inside. He hesitates, glancing at the cow again as though waiting for her to pull a gun on him or otherwise accost him, then sidles through the door.

"Whose cow's it?"

"I don't know. Brown's most likely. I haven't called down to the barn yet. I just got home a few minutes ago. Want something to drink?"

Winston smacks his lips.

"What would you like? I have ...," I poke my head into the fridge, "Chardonnay, OJ, milk or water." The milk's been in there awhile. I sniff it. "Skip the milk."

"OJ's good," Winston says. Then, "Hear about the manhunt for your dad?"

All the blood that previously coursed unnoticed through my hands suddenly flees. I drop the carton of juice, narrowly missing my foot.

"What?" My voice is small. I clear my throat. "What are you talking about?"

Winston nods, rubs a calloused hand over his head making the hair stand up even more.

"Sorry, Tatum. I heard about it on the scanner just now. No good. No good at all." Winston is shaking his head. I curse the fact that my own scanner is dead and has yet to be replaced.

"I just saw him." I stoop to retrieve the carton from the floor then pour the juice, setting the glass down in front of my elderly neighbor. Maybe a little too hard.

"Sorry," he says again.

"What did they say? On the scanner?"

Winston stares at me blankly. *Don't check out now. Please.*

"Winston. What did the police say on the box?"

He gulps juice. A little misses his mouth and dribbles down the side of his chin then onto his t-shirt collar.

"Huh?"

"When you heard about my dad on the scanner, what were they saying?" I repeat.

Winston rubs his hand over his head again, looks across my living room to the back deck. "You started seedlings yet?"

I groan. Despite his near genius at electronics and repair work, Winston is a few flies short of a full tackle box. Talking with him is frustrating at best, infuriating at worst. My hands are still shaking, and I want to grab the man, shake the information loose from his memory. It won't do any good I know. There have been plenty of times over the past couple of years when Winston's memory has failed. I've never wanted it to come through so badly before.

"No, no seedlings yet. It's only mid-fall. I won't put any in till February probably." I pour myself a glass of water and gulp some down. "Are you sure you don't remember what was said about Jack?"

"I gotta get back home," Winston says, draining the last of his juice. He licks the remaining drop off the rim and gives me a salute. "Got the hogs waitin' to be fed."

Winston grew up on a farm and in fact, still lives on the same land his father and grandfather before him tilled. But there haven't been any livestock on it for decades. A couple stray dogs and cats that Winston can't bear to turn away are the old homestead's only animals.

I walk him to the front door. *Please, please remember.*

He stops on the front step. He's remembered! Gazing at the cow, he turns and offers me a lopsided smile.

"You gonna build a barn for that thing or what?"

I shake my head.

"Maybe I'll walk down to Brown's and let him know."

"Faster to call him," says Winston, who doesn't own a telephone himself. Convinced that the government is listening in on calls going to and from his house, he cut his own phone lines years ago. Now it's just him and his ham radio, an emergency scanner and an ancient phonograph. "For when the Dark Times come," he says.

"My place is going to be the social hub of this town when there's no more technology."

I've just re-settled myself on a bar stool when Winston pokes his head back through the door. "Don't forget to plant pumpkins this year, Tatum. Your seedlings are going to need to go in early on account of the late frost expected." I nod absently, wave a hand over my head acknowledging his nonsensical comment.

"U01. That's the code they gave for your Dad on the box. G'night."

I sit, tracing my finger over the stain my coffee mug left this morning. My finger is trembling, and my gut feels that familiar hot, tight sensation that it gets when something really bad happens. Fleeing or evading police or a roadblock, that's what the code means.

Crap.

CHAPTER FIVE

It's after nine o'clock on Thursday night. Darkness presses against the windows, and I want nothing more than to pull on flannels and cozy up in bed. Instead, I'm standing over the bathroom sink, pasting fake eyelashes on, and being careful not to get water or leftover toothpaste on my thin red sweater. No, I don't have a third career as a go-go girl. I'm going to see if I can find my new buddy Walter. Mary Ann pulled through, providing me with the documentation and cash yesterday morning.

The last edge of lashes has been glued down. Not bad. The wig is dark blonde and has long, soft waves that look real. It's one of my most recent purchases and is made of human hair. It cost a bit, but it's worth it. Living near a small town in a small state, it's easy to bump into people you know. I can't afford to have my cover blown. My lips are cherry red, and my freckles are covered with a thin layer of foundation. I pucker, then grimace, and make my eyes go wide to make sure everything stays in place.

Satisfied, I go back into the guest room-turned-dressing-room and look through the racks until I find black boots. The pointed heels look deadly, not a bad thing considering where I'm going. I slither into a knee-length clingy black skirt, covering the red sweater partially with a wool jacket. Done.

I grab keys, handcuffs, a stun gun, and a canister of pepper spray from the ring by the door, then turn the thermostat down and check my cell phone on my way to the car. I'd called my buddy, C.J., at the State Police after Winston left, trying to dig up some information on my father but so far no message or return call. This is an oddity. C.J. is prompt to the point of pushy and likes things neat and tidy. If he has messages, they get returned punctually, even if that means he stays for another hour or two after his shift is done. He doesn't even have any overflow in his email box, a sure sign of his anal retentiveness.

The moon is half full, hanging in the navy sky like a milkweed pod when I slide behind the wheel. The brisk air makes little puffs of white when I breathe. The ride into St. Albans is uneventful, but I keep an eye on the side of the road for deer, which migrate this time of year. All I need is a totaled car to add to my financial issues.

Jazz station cranked, my thoughts turn to my father, but I steer them back to Walter. Butterflies dance in my belly, and I check three times to make sure I didn't forget the pepper spray, stun gun or handcuffs. Hopefully I'll only need the handcuffs.

The city is quiet as I drive through, occasional cars and trucks leaving stores along Main Street. Taylor Park is well-lit and pretty, vintage looking strings of white lights outlining some of the mature trees. I take a right onto Lake Street then another onto Catherine Street. No parking outside of The Trap which is throbbing even at street level with a loud bass. I circle the block twice and—lucky day!—a spot opens at the end of the block just as I go around the corner. I park, lock the car and start walking. The air feels icy on my bare legs. As I approach the building the music changes into a country song. Two guys wearing hooded sweatshirts slouch near the door smoking. One of them looks me up and down.

"Hey—" he starts.

"Not in your wildest dreams," I retort and walk down the stairs from street level to the basement bar below.

A muffled curse follows me into the bar. It's warm and dimly lit and smells like old beer, B.O. and cheap cologne. It still surprises me, walking into a place like this and not having a cloud of cigarette smoke hanging in the air like fog. Vermont banned smoking in all public places, bars included, in 2005.

Three beer-bellied men, two of them fringed with gray beards, watch my entrance. One says something I can't hear over the lovesick singer whining about his dead dog and jabs an elbow into Beer Belly #2's side. My teeth clench, but I remember that I'm not here as Tayt but Veronica, a blonde bombshell who needs to be nice, flirty, and most importantly, exceptionally fascinated by Walter Hawk. This will take all my acting skills.

I walk to the bar after leaving my jacket on an already full hook near the door, and cast what I hope is a flirtatious glance at the trio. One of them grins back, showing me a row of nubby raisin-like teeth. The two others just stare, as though I'm a bone and they are very large, very hungry dogs.

"Hey, how are you all tonight?" I call to them,

pressing myself close to the bar and flip my hair over my shoulders. Raisin Teeth grins wider, giving a long, searching look at my chest. The other two nod. The one closest to me asks if I'm thirsty.

"Parched," I say.

"What'll you have?" He asks.

"I'd love a gin and tonic."

He whistles through his teeth which are healthier looking than his buddy's. This one is wearing thick glasses and sporting a mullet, heavily peppered with gray. His eyes shift from one side to the other, almost in slow motion, giving him a comical, half-asleep look.

"Like the hard stuff, hey, missy?"

I smile.

He motions to the bartender, places my order over the booming bass. The jukebox in the corner, I realize, is supplying the outdated music. Apparently there's some sort of standoff between a hip hop lover and a country western fanatic. Vanilla Ice is yelling fast and loud as I survey the rest of the room. There are a half dozen round tables, most of them full. The carpet is an indeterminate color, stained dark in some areas, and I bet money, if I touched it, my hand would stick. Lighted signs announcing various beer brands are thrown on the walls in no apparent order, some hanging precariously, as though the slightest bump on the plaster surfaces will knock them down. The bar itself is small and crowded, the bartender a big, balding guy wearing overalls and a dirty apron. He puts my drink together and slides it toward me, nodding as Shifty Eyes tells him to add it to his tab.

"Thanks," I say and take a small sip. The gin travels

in a warm path from my lips to stomach and my shoulders relax a millimeter.

"Pleasure," Shifty Eyes says. "So what brings a beautiful lady like you to a place like this?" The other two beer bellies lean closer, Raisin Teeth smiling hopefully again. I hold in a shiver, shrug my shoulders.

"I'm new in town. Thought I'd check out the local nightlife. Plus, I'm looking for someone. A distant relative. Heard through the family grapevine that he might hang out here." I take another small sip of my drink.

"Who's that?" Shifty Eyes is apparently the spokesman in the group.

"Walter Hawk."

Silence.

"Great Uncle Walter," I say, filling in the silence and praying that I look young enough to have a great uncle in his mid-sixties.

The trio takes turns glancing at each other.

"Do you know him?"

"What do you want with him?" Beer Belly #3 speaks for the first time. His voice is rough and rusty.

I shrug. "Just to say hello. Is that a crime?" I laugh, but even in my own ears it sounds forced. "You know him or not?" I ask, playfully jabbing Shifty Eyes in the bicep. Leaving my hand there a moment, I note that there is movement toward the back of the bar. A card game at a small table. Voices raised.

"Back there," says Raisin Teeth, nodding toward the card game. Beer Belly #3 gives him a slight shove and Raisin Teeth shrugs.

"What's the big deal?" Raisin Teeth says. "Think

she's dangerous or something?"

"Definitely not dangerous," I say, smiling. I take another sip of my drink and nod toward the group. "Just looking forward to seeing Uncle Walt, that's all."

I sit, shooting the breeze with the three men but keeping a peripheral gaze on the group at the table. Finally my drink is gone and I stand, nod at all three.

"Thanks so much, gents."

"Awwww, come on. Where you going?" Shifty Eyes asks, apparently frustrated that his five dollar drink is getting away.

"Family comes first." I give his shoulder a pat, walking past. The trio turns, facing the back of the bar and watches my progress across the room. The image of Walter from the picture Mary Ann gave me is burned into my brain. I hope that I can pick him out in the dingy light. Turns out I needn't have worried.

"I know it, Hawk. You're cheating." The voice is raised, angry. I walk more quickly to the table. A heavyset woman sits at one end, her finger pointed toward my soon-to-be bounty. Walter sits, smirk planted, one leg crossed ankle to knee over the other.

"Settle down, Bertha."

"My name ain't Bertha, for the hundredth time. It's Claire!"

"Sure, sure. It's just," Walter sits forward, uncrossing his legs and stretching them out under the table, "well, you look like a Bertha to me. Big Bertha." This gets him a few chuckles around the table. The woman's face gets even redder, and I expect steam to erupt from her ears.

"Just shut up and play," a man says across the table.

He's wearing a polyester shirt with too many buttons undone and a pair of aviator sunglasses. He looks me up and down as I approach.

"Well, well. Who we got here?" Necks crane, and there are greasy-looking smiles from around the table. I smile and bat my eyes a little.

"Room for one more?" I ask.

Walter pulls out the chair nearest to him. Pats it.

"Room right here, sugar."

I smile again, scoot into the chair. My skirt hitches up on my legs, a detail that Walter does not miss.

"What are you playing?"

"Poker," Claire says, sulking from the other end of the table. She pushes herself back and her chair groans. "Least we was. I ain't sitting around for anymore of this." She points her finger again at Walter. It's trembling slightly.

"Yeah, yeah, Bertha. Blow it out your. ."

His voice is cut off by a new choice on the jukebox. Johnny Cash is singing about Fulsome Prison blues as the guy with the sunglasses deals the cards. I'm not a big gambler, but I have played a few times at the Montreal Casino.

Everyone around the table checks their cards, and I watch faces. Less experienced players scratch their noses or start rolling their necks or take a sudden interest in surveying the crowd. Veterans sit without moving, or if they are moving I can't see it. Walter spreads his cards out a few minutes later. "I've got a royal flush."

"I told you!" Claire screeches from across the table. "Where'd those cards come from, anyway? He loaded the deck." She struggles to her feet, assisting herself with a cane. "I told you he was cheating. How many times does that make?" She asks, looking around the table. No one makes eye contact.

"Go on home, Big Bertha. If you can't play nice, better not to play at all." Walter smiles, leaning back in his chair.

For a minute I think she's going to launch herself across the table, cane flying in front of her like a sword. Instead she turns, limps off toward the bar, calling insults over her shoulder.

A hand snakes around my shoulder.

"You want a drink, sweetie?" Walter's breath is hot on my neck.

"Oh, no. Thanks."

"No? How about something else then?"

A handgun? Preferably big and loaded?

"What did you have in mind?" I hope my voice is coy. I look at him from between my extra-long lashes.

"Oh, I don't know." He waves his hand around the room. "Splitting from this joint and getting a bite to eat. Or maybe doing something to work up an appetite first." He chuckles, and I realize how close he's gotten when I feel my ribs vibrating. His right hand is pawing my shoulder and the top of my arm while his left rakes the loose money from the pot toward him.

"What do you say?" His breath is hot against my neck and smells of old cigarettes and unwashed teeth.

My hands are clammy, and my heart has started beating hard. I feel slimy where his hand is touching me. Better to get him closer to my car, without all his pals around. Yet the self-protective part of me wants to elbow jab him and stick my fingers in his eyes.

"Sure," I say instead. "Sounds great."

We're just gathering jackets at the front door when Raisin Teeth dismounts his bar stool and walks in our direction. *Crap.*

"Sonny, what's up?" Walter calls, sliding his arm into the leather coat. "Didn't see you come in."

My heart is hammering, and my hands start to tremble.

"Just bought your girl here a drink," says Raisin Teeth. "Purty little thing, isn't she? Must be good genes run in your family."

Walter smiles and nods, glances at me, then his eyebrows pull together in confusion.

"Good genes do run in my family. Not sure what that has to do with this one though," he jerks his head toward me. I sidle up alongside him, hold his jacket so he can slip his arm through the other hole and smooth my hand over his chest.

"Let's get out of here, huh?" I smile and flutter my eyelashes again.

"Sure, babe, sure." Walter chuckles and gives a one-armed wave to the room in general. "Catch you all later. Be good now." He nods at Raisin Teeth who is watching us, his mouth slightly open. I turn and move toward the door and feel Walter's hand, warm and heavy, on my bottom guiding me out.

CHAPTER SIX

We walk to the car slowly, Walter's arm finding its way around my shoulders like a cloak. I'm still trying to get my breath back to normal, inhaling the night air which is crisp and intoxicating after the stale air inside. Stars above look like Lite Brite pegs, white points pushed into a velvety black background. A breeze swirls leaves around our feet. Walter's not much of a talker, thank God, but he is a smoker. He lit up before the door closed, and the smoke wafts into my face every several steps.

"So, where you takin' me, sugar?" Walter asks, following another drag on his cigarette.

"Oh, you'll see." My voice is honey sweet, and I smile up at him. He's bigger than I thought, all long legs and narrow waist. He's not put on the weight of a typical middle-aged man. Instead he's sinewy and hard looking. I debate the best way to approach this situation. He's not wearing a gun, unless he has a leg holster. I checked his sides and back while he donned his jacket. Still, he's got fifty plus pounds on me and about a foot of height. I finger the handcuffs in my coat pocket, make sure that one is open. My other hand caresses the stun gun.

"This is me here," I nod toward the Toyota. Walter snorts.

"That piece of crap? We should have taken my truck."

"Now Walter," I say, smiling up at him, "A girl's got to keep her safety in mind. I mean, I hardly know you. I can't just be driving off to God knows where, can I?"

"We'll change that soon enough, babe." He murmurs, drawing me close to his chest. His jacket is scratchy against my face, and I can feel hard muscle beneath. He tosses the cigarette aside and with the same hand, begins to grope at my chest. I clench my teeth but put a fat smile on my face.

I give him a gentle shove toward the car, and his butt lands against its side. I hold him there with my left hand, lower my chin and look up at him through my false lashes. Do guys really go for this?

Apparently. He starts moving his hands toward my chest again, but I bat one away playfully. The other, I grab with my left hand and without overthinking, whip the handcuffs out of my right pocket, snap one over his wrist and jerk him sideway.

"Hey, what the ...?"

Before he finishes the sentence, I've snapped the other cuff over the car's door handle.

Walter bellows curses. I tune him out.

Now comes the hard part. Ninety percent of the time I'm successful in these types of situation because I have one thing in particular going for me: the element of surprise. I have a couple of ideas of how I can get him, relatively unscathed, into the small sedan. But will one of them really work?

"We're going on a little field trip, Walt. There's

someone I want you to meet."

"No I ain't," he jerks hard against the cuff, his free hand snaking out fast and nearly connecting with my face. I step back, but he snatches at me again, nearly grabbing a fistful of hair. I move another step away. My breath comes in little clouds. The street is deserted, and I hope it stays that way.

"Your wife stopped by for a little visit with me. Seems she's tired of being used as your punching bag and is ready to see you get a little taste of your own medicine." He interrupts with a stream of curses, his voice raising an octave with each one.

I free the stun gun from my pocket, take a step closer and raise it toward his neck. Instinctively, he jerks his head back, eyes wide.

"What do you think you're doing?" He snarls at me, wrenching his hand hard. *Please, please let the door handle hold.*

"I don't want to give you a jolt, Walt, I really don't. I mean, I've got nothing against you personally. It's just that I took on this job, promised I'd deliver you to a certain spot and right now we've got," I glance at an imaginary watch, "just about ten minutes to get there. So, I'm giving you a choice. Either you calm down and get in the car or I will hit you with this." I press the button and the gun gives off a loud, sharp crack, a blue arc of electricity snapping. "You'll pass out and pee your pants, and then I'll haul you there in the backseat unconscious. It's up to you."

Walter licks his thin lips, glances down the street. Hoping for a buddy to walk by? I'm feeling antsy myself. All I need is for a black and white to patrol the street. I tap my foot impatiently.

"What's it going to be, Walter?"

"Fine. You win." He says. "But get that thing out of my face."

I smile. "You're smarter than you look. Now, be a good guy and turn around so I can fix the cuffs."

I snake a pair of ankle cuffs and chain around both feet first, then carefully, with the stun gun pressed against his neck and my thumb on the button, I use my other hand to unlock and then relock both hands together behind him. I grab a reusable cloth grocery bag from the trunk and stick it over his head, tying the loop handles closed around his neck—not tight enough to choke him—just so that he can't see. Then I push him into the back seat until he's lying, half-prone across the width of the car.

Walter isn't happy, curses at me every few seconds and complains that his arms hurt, his wrists hurt and dammit, he's going to hunt me down when he's free again and slice me from nose to toes. I turn the radio up loud and pay extra careful attention to the speed limit.

Twenty-five minutes later, I follow a pocked dirt road to a farm in Fairfield. It's been months since I've been out here. A cow pasture turned makeshift parking lot contains thirty or forty cars, trucks and SUVs. The Toyota nearly falls into a spot near a black truck. What if I can't get back out of this crater? I adjust my wig, take a deep breath and exit the car. I'll have to worry about it later.

Extracting Walter from the backseat is a load of fun and nearly twisting my ankle on the way into the old barn only adds to my pleasure. Irritation is crowding out the fear, and by the time we reach the barn door, Walter's voice has raised to near fever pitch of cursing and threats. I grab the bag from his head and smack him across the face, hard. "Would you shut up?!"

He looks ready to bite, but then the big door opens, and a man dressed in flannel and denim motions us in. I pay the cover charge of twenty bucks while the farmer stares at Walter's handcuffs. I'd removed the leg chains; it's hard enough to maneuver a cow pasture with both feet free.

The man points us to two other men, also dressed in denim, who guide us silently to the barn's interior. The silence is overpowered with screams and laughter and the sound of heavy bass as we enter what would have been a hay loft. Now, a circular area in the center of the hay-strewn floor is roped off with chain. Bodies of every shape and size, and faces mostly in their mid-thirties and older, crowd the chained area.

Walter takes an involuntary step back, his Adam's apple bobbing.

I smile up at him.

"Ever been in a pit fight before, Walter?"

I remove the cuffs, trying to be discreet. It doesn't matter. No one is looking at us, all eyes instead trained on two beefy guys in the ring. One has a bloody nose which has leaked all over his t-shirt. The second is sporting a swollen shut eye. Both have red marks covering parts of their arms and faces. They look exhausted and the one with the swollen eye ready to collapse. The crowd cheers as the fighter with the bloody nose plows a foot into the other man's solar plexus.

Drinks are passed in red plastic cups, no glass

allowed in the barn. Smoking is prohibited as well, not out of concern for health, but because the ancient structure would go up in a blaze in minutes if a fire started.

I leave Walter, who is mesmerized by the men in the ring, and move across the barn to a man who is simply called, "The Keeper." He holds a nearly full cup and barely glances at me as I approach. I turn, positioning myself so that I can keep an eye on Walter.

"I have a name to be entered."

The man nods but says nothing.

"Who is the best fighter tonight?" I ask, nearly yelling over the loud music and raised voices of the crowd.

"Bob the Slob, without a doubt." The Keeper says this with a straight face, and I try not to burst into laughter.

"What's that, his stage name?"

"Nah," the man rubs a calloused hand over his neck then gives it a crack loud enough to be heard over the music. "Nickname he never outgrew. Big boy all his life but just recently—last two years or so—he started weightlifting and took up weird-assed ninja fighting classes. Now you don't want to call him Bob the Slob to his face. Might be the last thing you ever say."

I smile.

"Perfect. My boyfriend," I point in Walter's direction. I can practically see his Adam's apple bobbing and hands trembling from here. "He'd like to fight Bob."

The man looks me over head to toe and finishes with a squinting stare in my eyes.

"That so."

"Yeah. Is there a problem?"

My breath is getting tangled in my lungs, and I have to remind myself to slow my breathing down.

"You think I didn't see you pull cuffs off that guy a few minutes ago?" The Keeper nods in Walter's direction.

Sweat breaks out along my backbone, but I don't break eye contact. I lift my chin.

"I'm putting two hundred on Bob if you make the fight happen. Three hundred if he knocks my, uh, boyfriend out."

The man smiles and opens his hand, palm up. "Hate to see how you treat your ex-boyfriends," he says with a rusty chuckle.

CHAPTER SEVEN

The next morning I stand at the office window looking out on the empty street below. The liquor store is dark, the barber shop and minimart are open, but business is slow. I stretch, reaching hands over head and let out a big, satisfying yawn.

It was nearly midnight before I'd stripped out of my hooker-wear and then showered twice with extra hot water. The shower was chased with a mug of tea laced with bourbon, and then I finally felt warm and clean enough to climb into bed. My dreams had been filled with erratic movements and faces in shadow until finally, blissfully, I'd entered the blackness of REM sleep.

I'd left an unconscious Walter at the curb of the city's hospital. He was still breathing when I dragged him from the car, a feat that left my back sore. Walter, it had turned out, wasn't quite so brave when facing a man fully capable of kicking his ass. A lot different to try to fight someone who matched you in size and exceeded you in strength, I guess. I think of Mary Ann—the photos she'd shown me of a bruised and battered woman barely recognizable—and the second part of the payment that's waiting for me and smile wide.

Returning to my desk, I flip through the notebook

that I keep in my top drawer. It's a handwritten log. *Well done* marks one column, the other half of the page reads, *Needs improvement.*

I think about last night, what I did right and what I should have done differently. No hovering middle manager or annual employee assessment to gauge your performance when you work alone. I love this about working for myself. But it's also easy to fall into bad habits and get lazy, and I don't want that to happen.

The whole evening went surprisingly well. I gnaw on my pen cap and then jot down a few notes. I should have worn protective gear. I have a set of Kevlar so thin it feels like long johns but is as strong as the traditional stuff. Luckily for me, Walter wasn't armed. Mary Ann told me that he never brings any of his guns along with him for a night out on the town. Still, better safe than dead.

Making a couple of other notes, I tuck the spiral bound book back into the drawer, find a place again at the window after starting the coffee brewing. The smell, hot and dry, fills the office. I sigh and smile in satisfaction. It was a good night, and the money will help float my office rent for another month.

I pour a cup of coffee and sip it quickly, but I can't enjoy it completely because of the niggling thought that swarms like a hungry mosquito. I look automatically to the big white house across the street. The window shades are drawn, and there is no movement. I decide to go over anyway, just to see if Alinah is around. Maybe Sarjana has come back, and I can at least cross that worry off my list.

I put a second cup of coffee in a ceramic travel

mug, top it with the silicone lid, then go across the street. The air is fresh and chilly, birds yak overhead about their daily to-do list, or whatever it is birds talk about incessantly.

I'm halfway across the porch when Alinah opens the screen door. She is dressed in jeans and a button down shirt that has a lot of intricate embroidery on it. Her hair is shiny and loose and flows around her face, which looks worried. She pulls the heavy wood door closed behind her, motions me to the stairs and around the side of the house. There's a small portico here, and we huddle underneath it.

"What's going on?" I ask. "Is everything OK? Is Sarjana back?"

Alinah looks at me. Everything is definitely not OK.

She shakes her head, presses slim fingers against her mouth.

"She's still missing?"

Nod.

"Have you called the police?"

At this, Alinah's head snaps up. She looks at me wildly, shaking her head.

"No, no. She be back soon. Doug, he real mad. But she be back. I know she will," she says it again, as though convincing herself.

"And you don't know where she went? Who she was with?"

Alinah leans against the post, eyes closed. Her breath makes a small cloud in front of her, as though exhaling cigarette smoke. She shakes her head, but this time it's slow. Tears are leaking from under her lids.

"Poor Sar." Her voice drifts off and her eyes look far away like she's looking into the past. Or the future. She looks old suddenly, old and tired. "I not know."

"Alinah?" A man's voice, quiet and low, sounds from the front porch. Alinah rubs her eyes with the sleeve of her shirt and smooths her hair down then gives me a wobbly smile.

"I go now. Doug, he call police soon if Sar not back. No worry, OK?" She smiles again and I nod, but my stomach is tight and hot.

"Let me know if I can do anything. And come over anytime if you want to talk or if I can help in any way. I'm working late today." I point at the building across the street and then feel stupid. She's been in my office once before. I fish a slightly wrinkled business card out of my pocket and press it into her hand. She doesn't look at it but nods and hurries back to the front of the house.

I hear the low rumble of Doug's voice, but I can't make out the words. Alinah answers him, but her response is drowned out by a delivery truck downshifting. I wait a minute then duck out of the portico.

I'm about to cross the street when I see my business card, crumpled, resting on a branch of the hedge outside Alinah's house.

"Hey Sleeping Beauty," a voice says, ripping me out of a fine afternoon nap. I jerk upward, a sheet of paper and pink Post It note stuck to my face. C.J. stands in front of me, hands planted on hips, his uniform snug and belly flat.

"Geesh, are you kidding me, Williams?" I say,

peeling the document and sticky note free and smoothing them onto my desk. "Can't I get a little peace and quiet around here?"

"Asleep on the job, as usual," he chuckles, then lowers himself into one of the client chairs, his long legs splayed out in front of him.

I grunt at him. I'm a grouch when I wake up. Even more so now because it was Mr. Anal Retentive who did the waking. My hands run over my hair which is sticking up in eight directions. "This isn't a dorm room," I tell him, pushing away from my desk and walking around to the front, checking the building across the street instinctively, my new habit. It looks quiet and still, window shades drawn.

"Thanks for answering your phone yesterday," I say. "I only called about eight times."

"It was two. And I was busy."

"Yeah, I gathered. What happened?"

"Can't discuss it. Important police business." C.J. stretches his arms overhead and then bounces his head, first to the left shoulder, then the right, a loud pop emanating each time.

"I'm not exactly a civilian here. I mean, I do have some credibility with law enforcement." I draw myself up, try again to flatten my crazy hair.

"Oh yeah, you do." A slow smile spreads over his face. "Especially with Rodriguez. He really thinks you're cute."

I roll my eyes.

"Do you have any information about my father or not?"

C.J. has a face like an old renaissance painting of

Jesus, all perfect and unblemished. Light brown hair, clear blue eyes, high cheekbones and flawless skin. But now his brow is furrowed, his eyes suddenly avoiding mine.

"Yes. I do actually."

"And?" I want to hear the words but at the same time want to throw my hands over my ears and sing loudly to keep them out.

"You might want to sit down, Tayt." His voice is quiet, gentle. This is worse than I thought.

"Oh for pity's sake! Just tell me already." I turn away from him but watch his reflection in the window's glass.

C.J. gets up. The easy limberness of his movements are gone. His body is slow, stiff. He gently pulls my shoulders around to face him. Standing, he towers over me. His broad upper half blocks the view of my desk chair which I suddenly wish I were sitting in. Despite the bravado my heart is hammering away like a jackhammer with an overdose of electrical current.

"We found a body, a woman."

I wait for him to say more, but he doesn't.

"And? What does that have to do with my father?"

"Well," he clears his throat, looks out the window then back at me. "There was evidence found at the scene. A cuff link with your father's initials on it. Tire tracks at the scene that match those of your father's car. And when the team searched his house, we found some clothing of his caked with mud. The same mud that was in that ditch."

He lets the words sink in. I'm nodding, but I don't remember how to breathe. My vision is wobbly and turning gray.

"Tayt?"

I continue nodding and then feel strong hands beneath my elbows. I don't remember slouching against the frame of the window, but here I am. C.J. leads me to my office chair and gently shoves me in. I slump forward, head in hands on the desk.

"When? Where?" My voice is small and my head remains cotton ball thick.

"It was early Monday, sometime between three and four in the morning.

The witching hour. A deep throb is starting between my eyes and around the sides of my head, over my ears.

"We got a call from an elderly man out walking his dog. Saw part of the body sticking out of a culvert and called dispatch." His voice continues in the same monotone drone. A vice-like clamp has formed over my chest, squeezing out breath. I feel hot and uncomfortable; saliva rushes to my mouth like it does before I puke. I sit back in the chair, take some deep breaths. C.J. is resting a hip against my desk, his arms crossed. He's studying me closely. Waiting for me to pass out?

"I'm fine," I say, though my voice sounds anything but. "Tell me the rest."

He shrugs. "We don't know a lot more than that. DNA testing is being done, but the results are slow. It will be two weeks at least before they come in. Another neighbor, further down the road, says that she saw your father driving like a bat out of hell around three-thirty in the morning. Was just getting done some overtime at her job. And then there's the fact that Jack ran from law enforcement. It certainly doesn't help his case."

"But that's all he is at this point? A suspect?" My voice has a high whine to it that annoys me. "What about him? Maybe he is another victim! Just because you found his cuff link and clothes with mud on it (yes, I realize as the words come out how incriminating they sound) doesn't mean that he murdered anyone. He was supposed to meet me the other night ..." My voice trails off, and I realize too late that I've let words spill that were better left unsaid.

"When did you see him?" Same monotone, but I notice C.J.'s back straighten even more than usual. I'm silent for a minute, two.

"Monday."

"When on Monday?"

I shake my head. "I'm not going to do this. I'm not incriminating my father so that you can arrest him for murder. You don't even know what happened yet. He could be lying in another ditch, dead, and here you sit playing God." My voice is too loud in my own ears. I stand up, and my legs are shaky. I'm not sure if it's because I still feel the need to pass out or if it's rage coursing through my system.

"I can't believe you! You knew this, and you didn't tell me before now?"

C.J. runs a hand through his hair, but before he can speak I jab toward the door.

"Out. Now."

He stands slowly, like a cat, but makes no move toward the door.

"Tayt," he says my name softly, and it's followed by a little sigh. "I don't want to arrest your father. We don't even know what's happened yet. But if you withhold evidence then you could be charged as an accessory in this, if it does turn out to be ... what we're hoping it's not."

"By who?" I practically snarl. "You? If your boss knew you were here, that you were tipping off an old girlfriend ... I know what you're doing and you can forget it. When you get a warrant and subpoena, come back and we'll chat. Until then," I jerk my head toward the door, "you know the way out."

I listen to his big shoes clunk down the steps and then nearly fall back into my chair. My hands are shaking as I reach to push the hair out of my face. *Oh my God. Oh my God. Is this really happening?*

CHAPTER EIGHT

Thoughts of my father are never far away, and I picture him now as he was standing in my office the other day. He looked so tired and uneasy. Disheveled. Unusual for Jack who has always been so perfectly groomed and in charge of things. I used to call him Mr. Immaculate behind his back, not only because of his appearance but because he acted like he was the product of the Immaculate Conception. The man that could do no wrong. Except he did. And then my worry morphs into anger.

This is oddly comforting.

I spend most of the afternoon shuffling papers around my desk, nearly sprinting to my car when it's time for a trip to Bakersfield. I'm going to meet with a mother who has been stranded with four small kids after her husband went "gallivanting" three days ago. She actually said that word as though he were a wild horse or a stray cat on the prowl. To be honest, "hired" may not be the right word. I accept a handful of pro bono cases each year, and Alice Wells is one of the lucky winners. There's another cleaning job on the docket, too, but that will have to wait until I get back from Bakersfield.

I ascend Fairfield Hill, Lake Champlain at my back and the sun hanging low in my rearview mirror. Trees flanking the road glow like candle flames: magentas, pulsing oranges and yellows so bright that the whole sky above seems to wave and shimmer. I crank down the driver's side window; the chilly air whips my hair around my head. I breathe deep. This is pure Vermont. The smell is unlike any other: a familiar mix of earthy loam, undetermined green things, sunshine and early snow blowing off the distant mountains.

A horn honking behind me pulls me out of my revelry. A dump truck close to my bumper gives another blast of its horn. I flatten my own hand on the horn but the piddly squeak that comes out is laughable. Glancing at the speedometer, I see why the driver is irate. But the hill is steep, and my sedan is old and tired.

"Give me a break," I mouth at the rearview mirror and motion with my hand for the driver to go around. He prefers to stay on my tail. I flip him off and am rewarded with another blast from his horn.

Fine.

I slow down even further.

He speeds up, nearly kissing the car's bumper.

"What is wrong with this guy?" My car whines in response, and for one horrible moment I think it's going to fizzle out and die. But it keeps going and finally the top of the hill is in sight. The dump truck swerves around me as we crest Fairfield Hill and then lumbers off. I flip him off again but doubt he can see me in the growing distance between us.

Jerk.

My thoughts stray back to my father, but I redirect them, pulling the directions out of my loose leaf notebook. I look up at the road every few seconds to make sure I'm not headed toward a ditch. I make a note of the next two turns but still miss the driveway for the Wells' homestead twice in succession.

The mailbox is collapsed into a wide ditch on the side of the road, and the driveway itself, dirt and gravel, is narrow and looks more like a cow path than anything vehicles regularly traverse. I nose the car down and follow it until it opens, slowly, to a clearing. In the center is a rundown house. More of a cabin really, with tar paper sides and so much junk around it that it's nearly camouflaged. There are two cars in various states of disrepair tangled in tall grass and a variety of rusted metal items that I can't make out strewn about the yard. Two ancient doghouses sit near the tree line, and miscellaneous clothing hangs from a dirty rope strung between two old maples.

One of the dogs runs out of his dilapidated house at my approach, barking loud and lusty. I sit in the car a moment. If I get out now, will this be the last time I walk normally? But then a woman's head pokes from the cabin's door and yells at the dog to shush. She motions me out of the car, a chubby baby on one hip. Another two kids tumble down the steps, and I see movement of a curtain in the window nearest the driveway.

"Alice?" I call out, tentatively extracting myself from the car.

"Yes. You must be Ms. Waters."

"You can call me Tayt. That's a big dog you have there."

Alice approaches, her steps firm and quick. She bends down and says something to the two small kids, and they laughingly grab the big dog's collar and haul him around the back of the house.

"Sorry about that. Old Buck is protective of me and the kids."

"No problem. It's good to have that safety out here, I'd imagine."

Alice nods. Her hair is a nondescript color, somewhere between dishwater and beige. It's pulled into a French braid that's coming loose. The baby on her slim hip pulls at her shirt which is stained and has a patch of something gummy-looking on it.

"Come on in." She motions toward the house/shack. "Let me get you something to drink."

We settle at the kitchen table which is also apparently a storage area, closet and countertop all in one. Toys and leftover cereal bowls complete with bits of dried on cereal mingle among toast crumbs, sweaters, a baby doll missing an arm and miscellaneous papers, unopened mail and books.

"Sorry about the mess," Alice says, sweeping aside enough of the table for me to put my notebook down. "I just can't keep up these days."

I smile, nod sympathetically, but my skin is crawling. The floor is dirty and sticky and piles of foodstuff, boxes and papers line every inch of the countertops. The stove is covered in dirty pots and pans. I'm aching to ask for a scrub brush and mop but refrain. Alice looks toward the coffeepot on the far wall, and I see that it, among the clutter and grime, is shining white and holds what looks like piping hot joe.

"Would you like a cup?"

"Sure, thanks," I say. I feel like I should offer to get one for both of us, but she's already opening a cupboard and pulling down clean looking mugs. She sets one before me and sits across the table.

"Cream and sugar?" she asks, then adds, "Oh, sorry. I just remembered I don't have either."

"This is fine." I take a sip and scorch my tongue.

I flip my notebook open, uncap my pen. The baby on Alice's hip dribbles something whitish and chunky looking from its perfect rosebud mouth, and I try not to gag. Alice doesn't seem to notice, and it's suddenly very important that I write copious notes on the lined page.

"So, your husband, Sam, can you tell me a little about his habits? Where he likes to hang out, who he spends time with, that type of thing." I sneak a glance up, trying to block out the baby, but the white dribble is still there. Before I work up the nerve to tell its mother, Alice bends her face forward, sees the mess and wipes it on the back of her hand. *Note to self: Do not shake hands upon departure.*

Alice sighs long and low; it ends in a sort of disgusted snort.

"I can't tell you where he hangs out. He doesn't tell me. But I know who he spends time with, most of his time. His best friend is Miller Stevens."

Groan.

I want to say, "Are you *kidding* me?" but hold it in. Miller Stevens is a notorious A-hole at the highest level. He's a convicted drug dealer, a raging chauvinist, and a bully who's been caught on animal cruelty charges more than once. Everything from cock fighting to leaving his dogs out in winter, all winter, without any shelter.

"OK," I say instead. "Well, that should make Sam fairly easy to find. If he's still in town, that is. Has he been in trouble with the police at all? Is this the first time he's done this sort of thing?"

Alice shakes her head. "No trouble with the cops I don't think. But yes, he's done this before. Not since little Lila was born, though." She glances down at the red-faced baby.

"Uh-huh. And Sam's been missing since when?"

Alice starts jiggling Lila, who's begun fussing, on her hip, and I worry that more of that awful stuff will come out. I shuffle my notebook onto my lap, just in case.

"He left late Saturday night while I was sleeping. Took the only car. It's a piece of junk but at least it works." She starts swaying back and forth as the baby begins wailing, its tiny face growing more red. I re-focus on Alice.

"Your only car?"

Alice nods. "I haven't been to the store in days. I got one sister, lives over in Enosburg, but she broke her leg a few weeks ago on the farm. She can't get over to give me a ride into town. And even if she could," Alice pats the squawking baby's back, as she nestles it up on her shoulder, "how am I going to fit four car seats in her Buick?"

Guilt twists in my gut, but I ignore it. I'm not the one that decided to start a hades daycare with a felon. Getting this woman to the grocery store isn't my problem. Besides, the kids look fine. Well, minus Poltergeist baby. They seem to have enough to eat, no nibbling on my arms and legs or anything. I re-focus on my questions.

"Does Sam work?"

Alice shakes her head again. "Got laid off more

than a year ago. Was working with Miller Stevens at one point, but then Stevens did a little time in jail for selling drugs so Sam lost his job there. Worked part-time at a gas station after that, but between paying for gas to get to and from work and the time it took, well, it just wasn't worth it. We get our state check, and I just try to make that stretch best I can."

"But he's not on disability or anything, right?"

"No. Not unless being an alcoholic is a disability."

"Is there anything else you can think of, places he talks about going or people he's maybe spent some time with? Does he use social media at all, like Facebook or anything?" Alice shakes her head to both questions and snorts when I mention social media. "He can't even use a computer," she says.

I close my notebook and re-cap my pen.

"I know where Miller Stevens lives and where he likes to hang out. If Sam is with him then I have a good chance of tracking him down. You don't think he'd go out of state, do you? Any family in another area that he might be staying with?"

Alice shakes her head and more of her braid comes loose. She reaches into a pile of papers on the table and fishes around for a few minutes. The baby has stopped squalling but is still whining, and the sound grates on my nerves. Finally Alice finds what she's looking for and hands a small photo over the table to me. It shows a picture of who I assume is Sam posing with a really big fish and a grin. A cooler half full of beer at his feet, the lake shimmering and blue in the background.

"No, he don't have much family left and what there is of it doesn't stay in touch." She smiles, tiredly, looking into the other room. "Otherwise, I might have a little more help around here at a time like this."

Oh for pity's sake...

It's my turn to sigh as I jingle my car keys. I really, really don't want to do this. But then the words pop out of my mouth, unbidden.

"Can I get you some things from the grocery store?"

Alice's eyes light up like Fourth of July fireworks. "Would you?"

I nod, and she moves to the counter and starts rooting through papers and piles of mail. I am most certainly going to regret this.

My phone rings before eight-thirty the next morning. Usually an early riser, I spent half the night tossing and turning, only finally able to fall asleep what feels like minutes ago. I'm half tempted to hurl it across the room, but then I see who the caller is.

"... lo," I say, trying to sound alert. Failing miserably.

"Tayt. I've got some information about your dad. I thought you'd want to know."

C.J.'s voice is brisk and business-like and I picture him at his office: back ramrod straight, shirt perfectly starched, feet directly under knees at ninety-degree angles under his desk. I sit up, rub some grit from the corner of my eye and shove hair back from my face.

"Sure," I say. "I'm ready."

I hear him shuffling papers, then a low murmur as another voice enters the room. The mouthpiece is muffled, and there's a moment of silence, then he's back on the line.

"Sorry, my boss was passing through looking for some paperwork."

My earlier anger at C.J. melts somewhat. He loves his job above all else, and I assume he could get into serious trouble giving me the information he's about to without going through the proper channels.

"Thanks," I say simply.

"You may want to hold onto your gratitude until you hear what I've got to tell you." His voice is low, quiet. I squirm into a sitting position, fingers tight on the phone.

"Your father was located yesterday in a bar in White River Junction. He was drunker than a skunk. Brought him to the jail up street for holding until the arraignment. He's being charged with ..." Here C.J.'s voice fails. I'm still trying to wrap my mind around the fact that my father was intoxicated. This has to be a first.

"... with murder."

"What?" The word rips through the room like an explosion.

"It gets worse."

My mind is spinning like a kaleidoscope. "How can anything be worse than this?"

C.J. sighs. "Apparently, the young woman that was found in the culvert? She was engaged in sexual activity before she was killed. Not sure yet if it was rape, but your father has scratches on his arms, his forearms, conducive to the victim struggling."

Pause.

"I'm sorry, Tayt."

I mumble another thank you and disconnect. A million

questions are swirling, bouncing around the edges of my
brain, but I can't formulate a single answer to any.

CHAPTER NINE

I drive to St. Albans later that morning, the previous couple of hours a blur. Winston stopped at the house before I left, making sure the car was running OK and suggesting some repair that would help with the loud squealing that started recently. I may have told him when I'd next be home, but I can't remember. I'd made breakfast with wooden fingers, then sat with it in front of me in the sunroom until it grew cold. I composted the untouched food and sipped too-strong coffee as I showered and dressed.

Woman.
Dead.
Culvert.
Rape?
Murder.

The words swirl around in my head, eddying and ricocheting off of brain cells until I want to scream. I can't think about anything else. But I must, not only because there's work to be done but because I will go crazy if I continue like this.

My first stop when I get into town is the county jail, housed in a renovated Victorian house with gingerbread trim. The dichotomy really is as odd as it sounds. My father, I'm told, is not allowed visitors at present. Also, apparently, he's still passed out. I want to ask permission to go in and shake him into consciousness, scream questions at him, but instead I calmly ask to be contacted when his next phone call is due. I leave my cell number, home number and office line. I call my mother next, sure that she'll be a frantic mess of tears, but I get no response. I leave a message for her and another one with my mentor, Judy, asking her to call as soon as she's able. If there's anyone who can figure out what happened Sunday night, it's her.

I arrive at the office on autopilot, pull out a new file folder and copy notes from yesterday's meeting with Alice into a new chart for Sam Wells. At first my movements are slow, clunky. As time passes, my brain starts to sort information, offer ideas on where to start with this case. I block out the image of my father every time it comes to mind, first every thirty seconds, then every few minutes until finally, I'm able to focus on my work.

Miller Stevens lives on a big spread on the shores of Lake Champlain. Here, farmland has been renovated into a golf course, a series of posh restaurants and some of the county's largest homes, mansions that are mostly hidden from view by abundant landscaping, maturing trees and privacy fences.

Staking out his house in the summer would be easier. A boat anchored in the lake near his house would give me access. But this time of the year a boat will look conspicuous. Unless one were fishing.

Ezra.

My oldest friend and one of the few people I know personally who had a childhood worse than my own. He answers on the second ring.

"Hey, where've you been? I thought you were going to call me the other night?"

"Yeah, sorry about that," I rub a hand over my face. "It's been a crazy week."

"Listen, Tayt, I hate to cut you off, but Father Benoir is going to be here soon and I have to finish a project for him—"

"That's OK. I was just calling to ask if you'd like to go to the lake tonight. Do a little fishing. Do you think you could borrow the boat?"

Pause.

"You? Fishing?" I can tell by his voice that he's trying not to laugh.

"I'll explain it all to you soon if you can come—I'll even pack dinner."

"Sure. Sounds ... intriguing."

"Meet me at the Bay around six, OK?"

Ezra mumbles a reply. I hear him greet someone in the room. "Sure. See you then."

Mondays, Wednesdays and Fridays I schedule time for Repo Renew, working around my caseload. It doesn't always work out that way, but it helps to have some semblance of a schedule. Judy returns my call before I leave for lunch and another cleaning job. We nix the small talk. With Judy this is the norm and to be honest, I like it. Time efficiency at its best.

I fill her in on what little I know of the situation. The fact that I've yet to have a conversation with my dad makes it a little difficult to be useful, but I relay the information I got from C.J., and we make plans to connect soon. My job is to get in to see my father, she says; her task is to start a case file and do some digging.

After a sketchy looking slice of pizza from the gas station across the street eaten in the car, I head back to the house I was cleaning Monday to finish the job. The afternoon is uneventful, and I blast the radio louder than necessary while scrubbing to keep my mind off the situation that landed my father in jail. A second phone call to the station goes unreturned. I finally give up for the day, stow my cleaning supplies and the trash bags in the car and head home for a hot shower.

The lake is spread out like glass when I arrive a little before six o'clock. Gulls have been replaced by Canadian geese overhead, and their honking fills the otherwise quiet air. I zip my jacket and pull on a woolen toque then sit on the hood, waiting.

Ezra pulls in, his big, dusty truck rattling. A dented aluminum fishing boat bounces along behind, hitting potholes. I smile and wave, and he waves back then lines the truck up with the launch and backs down. Hauling out the picnic supper packed into a red and white hard plastic cooler, I meet him at the boat.

"Hey, how's it going?" Ezra is tall, and he has to unwrap himself gingerly from the truck cab to avoid smacking his head. His face looks fuller than usual since he started growing out his beard.

"Not so great." I leave it at that and motion to the boat. "I'll fill you in when we're out on the water."

Ezra nods, raising an eyebrow, then does whatever fisherman-ly things have to be done to get the boat into the lake. Finally, he motions for me to get in, and I grip his hand and ascend. The small boat rocks, and for a minute I picture falling over the side. I grasp the edge with both hands, losing my grip on the cooler and watch mutely as it falls on its side on the floor of the boat.

"Easy, Tayt. We haven't even made it out of the bay yet." Ezra's voice is soft and I nod, gulp. He rights the cooler and nudges a puffy red vest with his foot.

"Why don't you put on a life vest?"

I debate for a minute. A life vest would make me feel a tiny bit better, but then I'll have to let go of the boat's side. Prying my fingers loose, I grab for the vest and stuff it on over my jacket, snapping the latches closed and resuming my tight grip on the boat. I may have just set a world record.

"You know we are still in only four feet of water, right?" Ezra's eyes are crinkled, and I shoot him a dirty look.

"I know that. Just shut up and drive this thing, would you?"

"Gotta grab the poles." He jogs back to his truck and returns with two fishing poles and a brown plastic tackle box.

"As if I'm going to fish," I mutter. "My hands are otherwise occupied."

"I noticed that. Which makes me wonder how you're planning to eat your dinner. Am I supposed to feed you?" He chuckles at this, and I grimace as the boat accelerates into deeper water. We motor along for several minutes. The air is bracing. My heart is hammering so hard I'm surprised that the life vest isn't jumping.

"Where are we going?" Ezra calls over the motor.

"You know where Miller Stevens lives?"

Nod.

"Head that way."

"A stakeout, huh? Starting to make sense now."
Ezra says something else, but the words are lost in the
wind. I close my eyes for a minute, the cold air whipping
my hair under the hat and snaking icy fingers down my
coat collar. But the smell is fresh and clear, the fishy
smell of the shoreline giving way to more pure air. If I
block out the part where we're skimming along water
many feet over my head, it's rather enjoyable. I picture
us on a sand buggy, racing across the desert. The safe,
dry desert.

Minutes later, the sound of the motor slows,
growing quieter. Finally, Ezra turns it off completely.
The only sound is the water lapping at the sides of the
boat. A serene sound, but it sort of ruins my whole
desert manifestation. I open my eyes. The sun is just
setting, red orb falling low over the mountains in New
York. For a minute, I forget about the boat and the
water. Cherry red mixes with a bright tangerine and then
slices of lilac smear through the sky. It's like watching a
watercolor painting being created.

"Gorgeous, isn't it?"

I nod then look over at Ezra. His gaze is on Miller
Stevens' mansion along the lake's shore. White pillars
open onto a stone patio which lines an in ground pool
and Jacuzzi tub. Landscaping prevents curious eyes from
seeing too much of the neighboring houses, but
apparently, Stevens didn't want to ruin the view of the
lake.

"I thought you were talking about the sunset."

Ezra turns, glancing over his shoulder. "Oh yeah. That's very nice, too."

I snort. "Aren't you a little materialistic to be a priest?"

"I'm not a priest. Not yet. So I have time to overcome my natural tendencies toward the desire of material things."

"Is that what Father Benoir tells you during confession?"

Ezra grimaces.

Father Benoir is the head priest at St. Anne's Shrine in Isle La Motte. "Old-school" is the term that springs to mind when you meet the man. Pious to the point of prickly. Not all Catholics are like this, Ezra has told me more than once. But Benoir's attitude rubs me the wrong way. I wish that Ezra had found a different place to serve as brother, but I'll never tell him that. Having him relatively close by encourages me to keep my mouth shut.

"So tell me what's going on," Ezra says, yawning, then grabbing a pole and digging through the tackle box.

I tell him about Jack and the dead woman and the drunken state that C.J. told me the officers found my father in.

When I'm done, there is only silence. Ezra's hand is still in the plastic box, not moving. His eyes are serious and dark, looking out over the last of the fading sunset.

"What can I do?" His voice is quiet, barely audible over the sound of the water slapping the sides of the boat. He looks at me, his eyes are pained, and I know it's not only for me but for himself. Ezra is like that: Your pain is his pain. A warm rush of gratitude gathers under my ribs.

I clear my throat, look away. There are emotions right up near my surface that I don't want anyone to see, not even Ezra.

"Nothing, really. Not yet."

"Is that why we're here?" He jerks his chin toward the Stevens' mansion behind us. I shake my head.

"No, this has to do with a case. Sam Wells—you ever heard of him?" Ezra ponders this and finally extracts bait from the tackle box.

"I don't think so. Should I have?"

"Not unless you're a low-life scumbag like Miller Stevens."

"Ah, then no. I haven't."

"He's my newest case, Wells that is, not Stevens." I fill him in on the details that Alice shared with me.

Ezra nods, says nothing.

We sit in silence for a stretch of time. I take turns clutching the side of the boat with one hand and zooming in with my camera's telephoto lens in the other. I stopped by the office long enough to drop off my notes and photos from this morning and to get my more powerful camera with a new zoom lens.

Ezra is quiet, just dips his line in and out of the water, glancing periodically from the place where the sun set to the house behind him. The lens helps. I can see into three of the main rooms in Miller's house—the kitchen, wide and open on the first floor, mostly made of stainless steel appliances, the great room which features a floor to ceiling fieldstone fireplace and on the second story, part of what I assume is a den or library. Books line three walls, the fourth is made of windows and overlooks the lake. I drop the camera to my chest, sit back for a minute, forgetting where I am, and dream about what it would be like to live in a house with that many books. Too bad it's wasted on the ignorance of the homeowner. Or maybe they aren't real books at all? Maybe his library is filled with cardboard imposters.

Finally dark falls, first on the tree line nearest the main road, then over the houses. Spotlights and indoor lamps are clicked on along the shore, little glimmers of brightness against the velvety blue of dusk. Ezra reels in his last cast, nothing to show for his hour's efforts. I smile at him.

"Thanks for coming."

"Wouldn't miss it. Seeing you in a boat? That's worth the effort of hauling it over here any day." He's grinning as he deposits the fishing pole back into the bottom of the vessel. My stomach growls.

"Sorry, I forgot about dinner." I nudge the cooler with my foot.

"That's OK. Let's eat when we get back to the parking area."

I nod, grateful since I don't have a third hand to hold my food, and my other two are occupied. I try not to think of the depth of the water beneath us as Ezra starts the boat. We're not even a hundred feet away when I see movement and hear voices coming from the back of the Stevens' house. I motion to Ezra, but he's already cutting the motor, letting the boat drift.

"Sammy!" A voice yells, low and loud. There's a muffled response, and then a figure exits a small beach house opposite the huge white monster. I grab my camera, focusing the lens as quickly as possible. The lens is so magnified that the picture shakes and jerks, and it takes several long seconds to determine what it is I'm looking at.

First I notice a dark red door, the exterior door of the beach house. Moving the camera to the right, slowly, I see something that makes my heart stop. A very large, very powerful looking telescope, trained in the direction of the lake. No, not just the lake. On us.

At the same moment, the sound of another boat engine starts, a powerful, low growl. The booming voice yells over it, "... in here!"

Sam moves toward the dock, pulling a ball cap low on his head. His hair is in need of a trim and sticks out around it like a fringe. The first man, the driver, is indistinguishable from the darkness around him. But I would bet money it's Miller himself.

"I think we'd better get out of here," I murmur, continuing to train the lens on the black boat. It revs its engine again and then pulls out hard and fast from the dock, headed directly toward us.

CHAPTER TEN

The light from the big boat blinds me momentarily. I shield my face with my hand which glows white in the darkness. Ezra's face is turned away. Calculating the distance to shore maybe?

"Can you get us out of here?" I have to yell to be heard over the hearty rumble of the other boat's motor.

Ezra shakes his head. "Not in this piece of tin." Still, he revs the small boat's engine and angles toward the shore, to appease me no doubt.

"Hey!" A voice from the boat yells. Ezra glances over his shoulder but doesn't slow. I continue clutching the sides of the boat, circulation nearly cut off. My fingertips are numb. The black boat continues to bear down on us. Fifty feet out. Thirty. Twenty. Then Stevens cuts the engine completely and skids in the water near us, the wake of the boat rocking our small craft as though it were made of paper. The engine on our boat stalls. I close my eyes and will myself not to scream. Panic climbs up my neck, choking me.

"What are you doing on my lake?" Stevens asks, his voice low and dangerous. He leans out, over the bow. His hair is dark and slicked back, mobster-style. He looks much the same as he did in high school, though the paunch and whiteness of his face are new to me. His left hand lifts a nearly empty bottle of Jack Daniels to his mouth.

"Wow," Ezra says, his hand on the motionless wheel. "You own this lake? I knew you were doing well for yourself, Miller, but I didn't realize you'd bought an entire body of water." His words are slow, a grin pulls itself up simultaneously.

I would have smiled myself if I could force the grimace off my face.

"Who's that?" Stevens peers into our boat, then barks, "Sam, give me the light." There's a shuffle and then the spotlight blinds us again.

"Well I'll be." Miller says. "Father Mannon, that you?"

Ezra gives a nod of the head, hand still shielding his eyes, left eyebrow arched. "One and the same, although I'm not a Father yet. Think you could get that searchlight out of our faces?"

Stevens chuckles. The sound is low and rusty. The light moves slightly behind us, and blue squiggles burst across my irises, dots swimming until my eyes adjust.

"Well, well. How are you, Father? I haven't seen you in ...." He looks off in the distance, as though the small island across the bay is going to tell him. "Well, it's been awhile," he says finally. "I'll always remember what you did for my kid sister. Nice of you to help our family out."

Ezra is silent for a moment. Then, "She was a smart kid and a good ball player. I was glad to write a recommendation for her. How is Lizzy anyway?"

"Oh, haven't you heard?" Stevens snorts, elbows Sam in the ribs. The smaller man winces but smiles along. *All in good fun.*

"Got knocked up at that prestigious school out in Michigan. Some deadbeat. Decided to keep the kid, mistake if you ask me. The last I heard she was at some rehab clinic, and her baby's in foster care. Yeah, she's a real smart kid, Padre. Real waste of time." He draws the word *time* out like it has three syllables. He takes another swig from the bottle and spills some on the front of his too-tight black t-shirt.

"And who's the lady?" Stevens motions with his hand, and the bright light pins me again like a bug. I picture my eyes with that deer in the headlights look and raise a hand to shield my face again.

"Hey, Stevens," I say. "Still as charming as ever."

"Well, well, well. If it isn't Little Miss Goody Two Shoes, Tatum Waters. You still dating Padre? I should have known. You two always were joined at the hip. Or maybe the lip," he gives Sam another jab. "Or maybe somewhere else."

Ezra, as though feeling the heat in my belly begin to bubble, nods toward the shore.

"Heading back in now. It was great seeing you both." First materialism and now downright lies? I should move before the lightning strikes. He cranks the key in the ignition and blessedly the engine revs.

"What's your hurry? I was just going to ask Tatum here about her dad. Heard he got himself into a mess of trouble."

I inhale sharply.

"What do you know about it?" I ask, my voice surprisingly steady.

"Well, I hear a lot of things around town, you

know? You can't move in the circles I do and not hear things. And what I heard was that your old dad got a little too rough during playtime. Killed a chink after he had fun with her." Another elbow in Sam's gut. It's hard to see the smaller man's face in the shadows.

"Nothing's been proven yet, you creep," I say. "And you can take your ..." The boat beneath me accelerates suddenly, and I nearly come off my seat. Ezra is angling toward the shore.

"Hold on!" he yells over his shoulder. As though I would do anything else. Craning my neck, I peer back. The bright light tracks us for a moment, dims, then wobbles uncertainly as the holder and the driver reposition themselves in the large craft. I hear Miller curse, and the sound of glass breaking, before the sound of the loud motor rips through the relative silence of the lake.

"You could have warned me," I yell to Ezra. He either can't hear me or is ignoring me. The wind whips through my hair, tangling it around my neck then sending it over my lips and nose. It itches, but I don't dare remove my hand long enough to push it away. The dark shoreline is drawing closer, but first we need to skirt a small island. I hope Ezra can see where he's going. The light on the small boat is dim and weak. I keep my gaze focused on the streetlight in the parking area. If I squint, I can just see a glimmer of the rusted truck bumper.

I look behind us again and gasp. The boat has gained on us. Its powerful motor rips through the water, spewing it out behind in a wake that could overturn the small fishing boat. I look forward again, hands white and clenching.

Come on, come on! My heart hammers hard and fast.

For a minute I think we're going to make it, but then Miller comes up alongside, and I see the malevolent grin on his face and hear his whoop. The nose of his boat is within touching distance if Ezra stretched out a hand. He doesn't. Both of his are planted firmly on the wheel of our boat which feels suddenly very much like a child's toy in an ocean.

"Awww, come on. Are you two leaving so soon?" Miller yells. With one fast motion, he cranks the wheel in the opposite direction, his wake hitting the near side of our boat. The water comes up and over the side, inches of it streaming in, wetting our feet and soaking our legs. It's cold and smells of seaweed and summer. Miller whoops again, and I see them circling back.

Our boat is still rocking and pitching from the motion of the waves. My stomach lurches, and then I spot the picnic cooler on the floor near my feet. It's overturned, soggy sandwiches and floating fruit bob in the water. Miller's big boat comes at us again, just as Ezra has circled around the island.

Almost there. Come on. As the bigger boat pulls around us again, I track its motion. When Miller again draws it in close enough to touch, I crouch, grab the small red cooler and hurl it as hard and fast as I can. It lands with a hard crack on the windshield and then bounces off into the undulating water. The crack fractures into a web of fractures. Miller curses. I grip the sides of the boat again, a small fissure of pleasure in my belly.

Miller yells a curse and then roars in once again. I feel rather than see what happens next. The boat taps the side of ours. I hear Ezra muttering under his breath or maybe praying, and then our boat tips, lurches sideways. Freezing water pours in. My eyes blur as water covers my face. The seat beneath me moves and jerks and then disappears. I scream as I fall, lake water covering my face and shoulders and then pulling me under.

CHAPTER ELEVEN

The temperature of Lake Champlain this time of year isn't anywhere close to the mid-thirties it will be in a few short months. Still, fifty-five degree water is a shock to the body. The lake is dark and loud. Sounds ricochet off rocks and shale underneath me, bouncing off and back, warbled. Everything in me wants to scream, to claw at the seaweed that brushes my face, but I'm paralyzed. For one long moment, I know this is the end. *Game over.* And then my puffy flotation vest does its thing, and I pop up to the surface, gasping in great gulps of air. Strong hands grab me, one clutching my vest from behind, the other secured around my shoulders. I struggle, pulling at the hands, digging in my nails.

"Ow!" Ezra says close to my ear. Then, "I've got you, Tatum. It's okay." I stop struggling but continue clutching his hands hard, letting him pull me along in the water. The stars above are reduced to dim pinpricks, the clouds smeary and dark. I'm shivering so hard my teeth are *rat-a-tat-tatting* together like snare drums.

"Tayt?"

"Wh ... what?" *Rat-a-tat-tat.* This is it. He's going to tell me something that he's been holding onto for years, some secret that is going to come out just moments before I die...

"You can stand up now. We're only in three feet of water."

I pitch forward, surprised, trying to make my floating feet find the lake bottom underneath me. He's right. My sneakers brush rocks and gummy sand. I look back and see the dinged fishing boat. Miller's boat is nowhere to be seen though its roar can still be heard farther out.

Ezra turns and swims back the way we've come, motions fast and powerful in the water. I crawl onto a large stone on the shore, pulling my legs out of the water. Water streams from my hair and old algae pools around the orifice where my ankles were, smelly and slimy. I sit and shiver and wonder if Ezra managed to keep his truck keys.

Ten minutes later, he's motoring the dinged fishing boat into the launch area. The side where Miller hit it is concave, a nearly perfect replica of the front of his boat. Ezra smiles at me, the whiteness of his teeth glowing in the darkness.

"That was quite an adventure," he says, shutting down the motor. "Got any plans for tomorrow night? Maybe we can bring wetsuits and do a little treasure hunting while we're in the lake."

I grimace, shake my head.

"Let's get you in the truck and find a blanket. I have a couple old ones behind the seat, I think."

I don't argue.

While he reverses the truck to the launch, I huddle in the mothball scented blanket and continue shivering. The whole event feels surreal; could a simple stakeout go any *more* wrong? What are the chances that Miller would not only see us but pursue us? And if Sam is staying there, what are the chances I'm going to apprehend him on the property? I snort at this thought.

T.R. Waters, Security Expert. Maybe instead my office door should say, *T.R. Waters, Bumbling Idiot.* On top of everything else, I've managed to lose my treasured Nikon and the beautiful new telephoto lens. Curses form in my head, but negative thinking and self-condemnation, while tempting, aren't going to change my situation. Besides, it's Miller's fault that all this happened, not mine. The thought warms me slightly.

A fly of a thought buzzes into my consciousness but is gone before I capture it. Ezra slides into the truck, asks for my keys. My hands pat both jacket and pants pockets and finally I find them. He hops back out after cranking up the heat then walks across the lot and wedges his tall frame behind my car's steering wheel, starting the car for me. I smile. Bumbling idiot or not, I know how to pick good friends.

It's as I'm driving home, darkness pressing against the car windows on all sides, that I remember what the thought was. Miller, when taunting me about my father, had said something about the dead woman. A racial slur, *Chink.* Could it be? I shut my eyes momentarily, the few images in my memory bank of Alinah's cousin appearing in quick, rapid frames like a jerky old-time movie reel. I open my eyes, watch the road, but in my mind I see Sarjana in a pink summer dress during the first weeks the girls had moved in across the street. Petite, dark like Alinah, not quite as striking but still beautiful. Her skin was darker, her hair short and wavy. Like a pixie or a fairy. Another image comes to mind of the two girls walking toward the house, hands clasped. A moment when they paused outside on the front steps, deep in conversation. Then the door had opened, a hand extended but no face visible. They'd both slipped inside. The thought makes me shiver suddenly, but I don't know why.

The next morning I wake up late, the sound of a chainsaw in the distance, buzzing like honeybees swarming. My body aches, leftovers from the adrenaline rush. I stumble out of bed. Is this how I'll feel every morning when I'm eighty? No wonder old people are always complaining. A hot shower helps loosen my muscles, and I grimace thinking about the gym. My workout last night was short and less than stellar, but I'm going to wait until later today and see how I'm feeling. At present I'd be lucky to hammer out two or three punches or kicks before falling over in a whimpering pile.

Dressing slowly, I steep a mug of green tea and pour it into a travel mug while watching the wildlife in my backyard. A brown bunny hops sporadically around the shorter grass near the trees while various birds sample bugs and who knows what else closer to the house. I tidy up the kitchen from last night, wiping toast crumbs into the trash and washing the few dishes in the sink, then grab my coat, wallet and keys. The car is cold and smells like lake water but starts without much complaint, and I drive in the direction of St. Albans City.

My first stop will be the county jail. I have to speak to my father. I make a mental note to call Mama again, too. Dreading it and pretending I won't have to be the bearer of bad news won't help me escape my fate. It's weird that she hasn't returned my call. Hopefully she hasn't heard about Jack through the grapevine and drunk herself into oblivion. Sam Wells needs my attention as well. I know now, at least, that he's at Miller Stevens, or was as of last night. I shiver again thinking of the lake opening up and swallowing me. A stop at the Stevens' place is definitely on the agenda and, on top of all of that, I should get out to my newest cleaning job, a seasonal camp on the lake. A property management-type gig I bid on and won. The owners have moved back south for winter, and this is my first job secured via Repo Renew's newly revamped website. I sigh, try to loosen the tight knot of anxiety in my gut.

The back roads in Hendricks Falls are beautiful but can be treacherous. Wet leaves line the edges, and the pavement itself is already glossy in places where early ice has formed. I slow down slightly, making a tight turn, then accelerate as I pass Brown's Organic Farm. A herd of Holsteins loaf near the fence, and one of them lets out a low moo as I drive past. Is that my old pal, Daisy?

The sun is just peeking through a thick wall of gray clouds when I pull into the parking lot of the Franklin County Jail. Unlike the large, razor wire-fenced state penitentiary on Lower Newton Road, the Victorian home-turned-prison houses the few suspects awaiting arraignments. If the cells fill up, overflow goes to the state pen, but I've never heard of it actually happening.

"How's it going, Mo?" I ask the elderly guard as I approach the door. He jerks upward from his stool, eyes bleary.

"Miss Waters." Mo is old-fashioned and prefers to call me by my proper name, though he insists I call him by his first. Maybe it makes him feel younger.

"I'm here as a visitor today," I say, handing over my business card and license anyway. Mo nods.

"Sorry about your father," he says, shuffling into the room and behind the scarred metal desk. He sits heavily there, then remembers what task he needs to complete and gets up again to make a copy of my documents on a huge and ancient copier in the corner. It squeaks and squawks but finally spits out a copy. He nods in approval and hands my cards back over to me. Next, he hands me a clipboard where I write, then sign my name and add today's date and the time of visit.

"You can go on back to the visiting room," he says, then moves toward the door marked "Reception," a throwback to the original house. Instead of a reception area though, I know what Mo will see. A long, dimly lit hallway with faded cabbage rose wallpaper falling off in some spots. Beyond that is a series of jail cells, old-fashioned with bars and zero privacy. Where before the rooms used to house a parlor, dining room and den, renovations over the years turned the living areas into four small cells.

I turn in the other direction, cross the large main room and go into an unmarked door which yawns open. Inside is a meeting table where three chairs from various eras huddle around it. I take a hard backed metal one and pull the seat in close to the table, back to the wall, eyes to the door. The air is stale and smells faintly of old ashtrays and perfumed chemical air freshener.

A few minutes later my father walks in, trailed by

Mo. I try to keep my face expressionless but am not sure how well I succeed. He's aged ten years, his hair is greasy, eyes smudged with darkness underneath. Instead of the usual perfect posture, Jack is slumped and bent as though carrying a heavy barrel on his back. His steps are slow and shuffling, and I wonder for a minute if he's in pain. But when he looks at me, I see it in his face. Not physical pain, but mental, emotional.

"Jack, what happened?" I say before Mo has even left the room. I had waved away the elderly man's suggestion that he wait outside the door and now he heads back to the front room.

My father is silent for several long moments. And then he does something I've never seen before. Shoulders shaking, his mouth twists, and then he's sobbing and covering his face with his hands, which are bruised.

"I think I killed someone."

CHAPTER TWELVE

The air is silent and still in the room, the only sound is the loud *tick, tick, tick* of an ancient and ugly clock on the wood-paneled wall.

"Tell me what happened," I say, the words sounding bossy and demanding in my own ears. "Everything. Please."

Jack collects himself, wipes his eyes on the back of his hands, leans back in his chair and looks up at the plaster ceiling, an ancient chandelier the only ornament. He's silent for several minutes, and then finally his voice breaks the quiet.

"The last thing I remember was talking with Simon in the barn on the night before all of this ..." his voice breaks. He clears it and goes on. "... before all of this happened."

"Wait. Back up. Who is Simon?"

He sighs then moves his eyes from the ceiling to a far corner of the room.

"Simon George is an old guy who was staying in the barn. He was homeless; I used to see him out collecting empties on the side of the road on my way to and from work. My car broke down once on my way to an important meeting, and Simon just happened to be nearby, helped me get it up and running again. He's a good guy, a veteran. He worked on tanks it turned out, so he had no trouble with minor car repairs. Anyway, we talked while we worked, and one thing led to another. The barn is empty right now, other than storage and my cigar room and den, and I figured why not? Just temporarily, you know. Till he found something else or decided to move on.

"But, I found out that Simon had invited other people to stay there, homeless friends. While I appreciated his concern, I wasn't running a shelter. The liability of having all those people in the barn was too much. So I went over that night to talk to Simon, to tell him that he'd have to be moving on."

"What was his reaction?" I interrupt, Judy's voice in my head. "Motivation," she used to say over and over. "Look for the motivation before anything else."

Jack glances at me, scratching his chin. "He was upset but not angry. More, I don't know, disappointed, I guess. Let down."

"And after that, what happened?"

"He offered me a drink. I haven't had one in months. I don't drink anymore, not since Max ... " His voice trails away, and he breaks eye contact, resumes looking at the corner. "Anyway, he offered me a drink, and I took him up on it. After he gave it to me, I knew something was wrong. I felt ... immobilized. Everything was heavy, all my limbs. I couldn't talk, and then I couldn't move. Then I blacked out."

"What?" My voice is incredulous, grating. "He drugged you?"

Jack wipes a hand over his face. For a second he looks ten years younger, but then he releases his hand

and his face sags back, lined and exhausted.

"I don't know, Tatum. I guess so. Why on earth he'd do that I have no idea."

I shake my head.

"Let's keep going. What's the next thing you remember?"

"I woke up in the barn; this was the next morning. At first I didn't realize anything was wrong. I fall asleep there sometimes, so it wasn't alarming waking up there. But my head, my head was killing me. I got up slow because of that, which is when I saw them."

Jack's voice stops again, this time full of emotion.

"There were these long scratches on my arms, deep enough to draw blood. And when I looked down I saw that I was naked. I found my clothes nearby, and there was mud on them, on my pant legs. And my boots, they were caked with it. I looked around the room, and I found ..." His voice breaks again, and he's silent for several minutes. "I found women's clothes all balled up in the corner, behind the couch."

"Chelsea's?"

He shakes his head.

"Chelsea and I, we've separated."

"And then what did you do?" I ask, trying to stay away from a topic that I'd rather not discuss.

"I panicked, I guess. I threw out the clothes, stuffed them in a garbage bag at the bottom of the trash outside, then I went to the house and showered. Three times actually. After that I drove around for a long while. I didn't know what to do. And then I went to see you. Remember?" He smiles at me sad and slow, and I feel like a fist is squeezing my gut.

"Why didn't you go to the police? I'm flattered that you thought of me, but shouldn't your first priority have been to report what happened? What you found?"

"I didn't know where to go. I was scared, Tatum. Driving around helped me think things through. No one could find me if I kept moving, right? And I figured if Simon drugged me then he must be working for someone or with someone, and I didn't want them to find me either. I just kept driving aimlessly, and then I thought that maybe you could help me. I know you've been working with that private investigator.

"But after I left your office I didn't know where to go, so I just kept driving around until I realized the car was nearly out of gas. I stopped at a station. I didn't even know what town I was in by this point. Anyway, I guess it was my unlucky day because a couple of troopers were just going in for coffee, and they must have heard the APB. They peeled out after me. I just drove. I drove as fast and as far as I could, and I couldn't stop thinking. The whole time I'm driving I'm just thinking about all of this and that woman, whoever she was, and wondering if I really hurt someone. I kept trying to remember, you know? But I couldn't. Everything was like a big, black hole."

He pauses again, runs his hands through his hair roughly, pulling at the ends until they stand straight up.

"Eventually I lost them, at a train crossing. I found myself in White River Junction, and I drove around there until I found a little bar outside of town, some dive. And I thought I'd just have a drink or two, just to take the edge off. And it helped. After the first two I wasn't thinking so much, and it didn't bother me that I couldn't remember what happened."

"Too bad you didn't stop at two," I say and then regret my words.

"Yes, too bad," he says. He leans forward on the table, drops his head into his hands. His voice is muffled when he speaks again. "I don't know what to do. I don't know what happened, and no one is going to believe that. No judge in his right mind is going to believe that I was drugged."

It was too late at this point, to do a blood test, but I didn't need to throw that cheery fact into his face.

Instead I say, "We'll figure it out, Jack, don't worry." More inane words had likely never been spoken in light of the situation, but my father looks up at me, eyes wet but tinged with an emotion that I recognize. Hope.

"Do you really think so?" His voice is quiet.

"Absolutely," I say, waiting for the lightning to follow my lie.

I call Judy when I get back to my car. My voice starts out haltingly, but telling her what's going on, laying out the facts, helps. It pulls the emotion out of it. She's quiet for several long seconds after I fill her in.

"Is your father an idiot?"

I'm so startled I can't think of a response.

"I doubt it," she continues. "First of all, he would have to be about the dumbest person on the planet to incriminate himself like this. The mud on the boots would be bad enough, but instead of just mud we've got tire tracks at the scene, a woman's clothes in his barn, not to mention a supposed eye-witness who saw your father's car fleeing the area in question."

This is news to me.

"There's an eye witness?"

"Come on, Tayt. You know how that works. Most of the time they aren't legit. Probably some neighbor with a grudge because your father's peonies are prettier, or he has a bigger boat." She chuckles at her own wit. "Do we know anything about this Simon guy?"

I give her the last name my father gave me. "Who knows if that's even a real name, though," I say.

"We don't have a lot to go on here, so let's start with what we do. If he is really a veteran, and he was with the army, at least we have a place to start." I picture her jiggling her knee as she's talking to me, her mind already working on next steps.

"I'll look into that. I've got an old army buddy that owes me a favor." The way she said "buddy" made me think that this person was anything but. "I'll get in touch with the detective up in St. Albans, too. I can also do a little digging on the identity of the woman."

Should I share my sickening suspicion that the woman might be my missing neighbor? I decide to, stressing the point that this is a guess on my part and that the source of the information isn't the most reliable. Judy makes an affirmative noise following my repeat of what Miller had said the night before, and I hear her typing away.

"In light of that, why don't you see what you can find out about her? Talk to, who was it, her sister?"

"Cousin."

"Right. Talk to the cousin again and see what she knows. If this is the dead woman, then the cousin should have been notified by now. Then find out what you can about the victim—family in the area, what she did for a living, all that general stuff."

We've slipped back into our old roles of mentor/mentee, and it feels comfortable, grounding.

"Thanks, Judy," I say, willing the emotion out of my voice. "I appreciate the help."

"No problem, kid. Keep your chin up."

She disconnects, and I lean back in the car's worn, comforting seat. That's a tall order on a day like today.

CHAPTER THIRTEEN

"Mama?" My voice is shaking, and I take a deep breath, exhale with the phone away from my head.

"I know why you're calling, Tatum, and you can spare me the excuses." My mother's southern drawl contains a smile, and I rub a hand over my eyes, wishing I wasn't the one making this call.

"You heard about your sister flying in and staying here, I'm sure. I just want you to know that you will appear at dinner tonight, like it or not. And you will be clean and presentable, understand Young Lady?"

Not Sophie on top of all this. A girl can only take so much.

"Um, that's not why I'm calling, Mama."

"No?" My mother's voice is still teasing. "Were you finally going to take me up on that offer for a girls' spa day then?"

I shake my head, then feeling stupid since she can't see me, blurt out, "Jack's in big trouble. He's in jail."

Silence.

I wait a few seconds.

"Mama? Are you there?"

"I'm here." Her voice is quiet, and I can hear the tears there. *Don't fall apart already. I haven't even gotten to the worst part yet.*

"What's happened?"

I tell her. It's hard to get the words out, and the tight band in my chest and gut are back. There is much weeping and possibly some gnashing of teeth on her end. Ten minutes later she's still asking me, "How? How can this have happened?" when I tell her that, though I hate to, I have to let her go. She sniffles, and I picture her running a perfectly manicured finger under each eye, carefully so as not to smear any makeup.

"Thank you for letting me know, Baby," she says. I'm about to hang up when she stops me.

"Keep me up to date on everything that happens, won't you? And Tatum," another shaky sigh on her end, "I'll see you tonight at dinner, won't I? Five-thirty sharp. At times like this, especially, we need to stick together as a family."

Ugh. The old guilt card.

"I have to work."

"But—"

"I'll make an appearance, say hello to Sophie, but don't count on me for dinner."

Another sigh, disappointed this time. I say goodbye and hang up before she can add in another plea for my attendance. As if dealing with Jack and this nightmare isn't bad enough, now she expects me to sit and chat with my older sister about her tremendous career, stellar financial bonuses and husband number three and how perfect they are for each other?

Give me a break.

I look longingly at my favorite deli, Big Daddy's Deli Delight, as I drive past but am already running late.

There's no way I can make a detour. Instead, I pull out a small box I keep under the passenger side seat, filled with energy bars and bottled water. There's another similar box in the trunk, though it's larger. That one contains a first aid kit, road flares, a rain poncho, an extra ball cap and God knows what else. Sometime I should go through it, I guess. "Sometime" is becoming a new mantra.

One hand on the wheel, the other rummages through the box until I find a peanut butter and chocolate chip bar and snag a bottle of water. The lunch of champions. I follow side streets, making right and then left turns, until arriving on Main Street in St. Albans.

I stop for a pink-haired teen in the crosswalk, and she saunters across the road, texting all the while. A group of gray-haired men in tweed coats stand in the park, pointing at the large green fountain. Putting my window down, I hear the church bells as the scent of coffee, frying fat and something sweet waft into the car. I munch on the stale bar, washing it down with water and wishing I'd had something more than tea for breakfast. My stomach whines, the smells reminding it of the unjust treatment.

From Main Street I bear right onto Lake Street, which turns into Lake Road, which eventually brings me out to St. Albans Bay. After that, the newly developed Lake Champlain Place, a stretch of approximately three miles of fine dining, a golf course, boutique shops and monstrous houses tucked behind privacy hedges.

I pat the canvas messenger bag on the seat beside me, making sure I tossed in my old camera. I won't have my super-powered telephoto lens this time, but an older, slightly scratched model will have to do. I also have a set of binoculars, an old floppy fishing hat and a wrinkled canvas vest that I hope will help me look like a bird watcher.

The sun is warm, and the air blowing through the crack in the window feels good. I smell the lake before I see it, a combination of seaweed and sand and freshness that isn't found anywhere but by a body of moving water.

I park alongside the entrance to Cohen Park, a town-owned beach that sports volleyball sand courts, a beach covered with shale, a playground and picnic tables. The gates are closed and locked now, the season over, but I doubt anyone will bother my rust bucket while I'm gone. I pull on the vest and hat, then sliding the bag's strap over my shoulder and across my chest, I start walking. I test out the binoculars on the way, adjusting the lenses to get a clear picture. A startled mourning dove flies out of a thicket of bramble, cooing its way up to a power line. As I get closer to the Stevens estate, I hear a flock of Canadian geese heading to their winter home in the south. Most people refer to them as Canadian geese, but Canada geese is the proper name, Ezra told me once. Stupid bits of trivia like this have a way of lodging themselves in my brain. I watch them for a few minutes, not only because of my cover as a bird watcher, but because they're fascinating. The V-formation breaks momentarily, and the birds rearrange themselves. Geese, Ezra also told me, can fly almost fifteen hundred miles in a twenty-four hour period if the winds are in their favor.

The breeze coming off the lake is chilly, nipping at

my nose and tugging at my hat. I pull it down harder on my head and continue on. Miller Stevens' mansion is ostentatious: white columns out front with a circular drive that frames a fountain of a naked woman clutching at her breasts and gazing at the sky. The stone is dry, the water having been turned off for the cold-weather months, but her hollow, unseeing eyes search the clouds. Maybe for some clothes. A black iron fence follows the front of the property, but the sides are open, letting people know that Miller isn't afraid of anyone sneaking onto his property. I've seen the Dobermans that he keeps. They are likely enough to dissuade most would-be trespassers.

Across the road from the three-story house is a small grove of trees. This property is as yet undeveloped and will make the perfect spot for spying. I climb down into the dry ditch and then up again, leaves crunching loudly underfoot. Walking into the grove of pine and spruce trees, I breathe deep. It smells like Christmas, and the feel of the sun on my cheeks and the sound of dry leaves scratching together overhead make me smile. The maple trees haven't yet lost their leaves, and their brilliant crimson color nearly glows.

I settle against one of them, back pressed into bark, and wait. I thumb through a *Birds of Vermont Guidebook*. Every actress needs a prop, right?

Thirty minutes later, there is still no movement in or around the house. The mail truck stops by, belching a puff of exhaust before moving on. My fingers practically itch with the desire to go snoop in the glossy white box. Instead, I change the position of my legs, stretch my arms overhead. Spying through my binoculars hasn't provided much stimulation. Thick drapes or fabric blinds cover every window facing toward the road.

I'm no slouch so sitting on my rear while there is so much work to be done is frustratingly hard. Give me a to-do list of seventy-five items, and I'll fly through them until I crash. Make me sit still in one spot for hours on end, though, and I come undone. Maybe Judy and I have more in common than I thought.

Pulling the binoculars up to my eyes, I study the nearby treetops. I recognize the sound of a chickadee and moments later see its tiny black and white body bouncing through the leaves. Its eyes are shiny, and for a second it cocks its head, as I try to recreate the *dee-dee-dee* sound that it makes. Then a door opens, and I forget about the bird and swing my attention and binoculars back across the road.

This must be my lucky day. Sam Wells is coming out of the house, followed moments later by one of the massive Dobermans and finally, Miller Stevens.

"... yourself!" he yells back at the door that's slammed shut behind him.

Sam grins, hand on the passenger side of a shiny black full-size truck. The word "Hemi" in big, silver letters graces the tailgate. Twin smokestacks poke up above the cab.

Miller flips a thick middle finger toward the door.

"Get out of here, Max." He stomps a foot toward the big dog which cowers then slinks back to the wide front porch.

"... up street first. Then maybe we'll see ... need some R&R, am I right?" Miller's words are being carried in the opposite direction by the wind. A volcanic laugh from Miller is answered by a slow smile from Sam. I crouch, crab-walking closer to the road and trying to stay low and inconspicuous.

Standing motionless on the step beside one of the thick pillars, the dog, Max, watches his owner spin out of the driveway, spewing gravel and swinging the truck's back end wide on the paved road. Heavy bass follows the truck, and I sprint from the nest of trees, staying in the ditch, hunkering low. The camera bag slaps on my hip and the binoculars bounce off my chest, nearly smacking me in the nose. I clamp a hand over them and run full force to my car, legs burning, then slide behind the wheel, not bothering to remove the bag or binoculars. I pull out from the parking area, wheels chirping on the pavement. I hope that Miller will slow down because there's no way that this ancient rust bucket is going to catch up otherwise.

It's not until we are in the city, stopped by a slow-moving freight train, that I catch sight of the big truck. The bass is still booming; I could rock out if I were so inclined from two cars back. Both windows are open, and a hand on either side of the truck flicks ash off of cigarettes. Or maybe joints. Then the train is gone, the rail gate lifts and the red lights stop blinking. Two blocks later, Miller swerves into a parking spot, and my breath freezes in my chest. He makes a U-turn at the liquor store then pulls up directly in front of my office building and kills the engine.

CHAPTER FOURTEEN

I speed past, then take the next right and circle around the block, trying to formulate a plan. If they're still in the truck, should I approach them or wait for them to follow me upstairs? I think about the fragile staircase and their big, heavy boots.

But when I nose the car in behind them, I see Sam trailing Miller onto the front porch of the house across the street. Alinah's house. She opens the door, and even from here I can tell she's upset. Her hair is matted, and her face is splotchy. She's wearing a faded flannel shirt pulled tight around her middle. Miller says something to her then rudely shoves his way in. Sam shrugs, gives her a smile, and follows.

"D-man, where you at?" I hear Miller bellow. Then Alinah pushes the hair back from her face and retreats back into the house.

I sit for a few minutes parked along Lake Street. If it wasn't me that Miller was going to see, there's no need to bring unwanted attention to myself. I drive around back to the parking lot. Same car still up on blocks. But it's been joined by a few others, these apparently in working condition. They probably belong to workers of the gas station down the street.

Finally, I pull the canvas bag and binoculars off,

stuff them under the seat and lock the doors, then pick my way across the broken concrete to my building. Would it be better to try and see what I can from my office window or sneak over to Alinah's house and listen outside a window? It's a little late in the season for any to be left open, though. I opt for choice number one and take the stairs quickly, unlocking the office door and re-locking it behind me. Pulling a telescope from the hall closet, I drag the tripod to the big window nearest my desk and set it up. Thank God Ezra used to be such a bird watching geek. I inherited most of his old equipment which comes in handy.

I train the glass on the window nearest the street but see nothing. I move to the others, scanning first the ground level floors and then the ones above. These are shuttered, all except one. There is dim light coming from it, and I adjust the lens of the scope, trying to clear the fuzziness from the picture. A back of a head. Doug, most likely. Beyond him are two dark figures, sitting too far from the window to make out features. Miller and Sam, I assume. I'm about to try to readjust the lens again when the figure furthest from the window moves closer. Miller's face is perfectly outlined. I wish that the telescope was a high powered rifle. Does this make me a bad person?

Keeping the lens focused on the window, I see movement. Miller's mouth is shut for once, so he must actually be listening to something that the other man is saying.

Where is Alinah? The image of her blotchy face and swollen eyes worries me. Has she gotten word that the body of the woman found was her cousin? Or maybe she's just worried about her. I think about my father's hands, *"There were scratches on my arms ..."*

Movement behind the window brings my attention back to the trio. Miller has turned, face back toward the other man. Sam, I assume. He nods in conjunction to whatever Miller said and Doug lifts his ball cap up, rubbing his crew cut hair underneath and then mashing the hat back down. Then he stands, hands on hip, back to the window. From the way his body moves it's obvious he's shouting something. The three men look toward the door which opens moments later. A young woman steps into the room, dark hair, long limbs, pretty. Her eyes are almond-shaped, but she's mostly looking toward the floor. Doug says something else and tosses an elbow jab into Miller's side. Miller grins back at him good naturedly then pulls the woman by the hand out the door into the hallway. She follows as though leashed.

Doug asks Sam something, but Sam shakes his head. *No.* He too goes out into the hallway and seconds later a light comes on in the front room closest to the porch. I wiggle down onto my haunches, training the telescope at the window closest to the street. There's a thin slit of visibility through the blind, and I see Sam hunker down on a low couch, the bottom half of him obscured from view. He has a can of beer in one hand and a small pipe in the other. Pot? Crack? Light from a television illuminates his face in a pale blue wash. He's alone in the room as far as I can tell.

Putting down the telescope, I rest my arms on my knees and sit cross-legged on the floor. What's going on over there? I need to talk to Alinah but don't even know what her cell phone number is. Does she even have a cell phone? I think about her explanation for being here in St. Albans, that Doug was Sarjana's boyfriend. He doesn't seem very upset about her disappearance.

A hot, sick feeling passes through my gut. *What if ...*

I put a quick call in to Judy.

"Did you find anything out about the dead woman yet?" I ask, barely waiting for her to get out a hello.

"Was just going to call you, Tayt," Judy says, her mouth half full. "Hang on." I wait impatiently while she finishes chewing and swallowing then hear her take a quick sip, diet Coke I imagine, before she speaks again.

"Weird thing is that there are no records so far, not since she entered the country three years ago. Malaysian passport, all legal. But since then, nothing: no address, no phone number, no driver's license or taxes filed. It's like she was, I don't know, invisible."

"Can you give me a name?"

"Sure. My source had access to a partial of the autopsy report. Let me grab a copy. I don't have this, by the way, not legally at least, so don't think about being able to use it for your Dad's case."

Paper rustles, and I imagine Judy, reading glasses perched on her nose, surveying the data with one finger tracing its way down the page. How many times had I seen her do this while working in her office?

"Sarajana ... woo, I don't know how to pronounce this last name," Judy says. "Sarajana binte Budiarto. I'm probably murdering the pronunciation."

I'm gripping the phone tightly and don't have enough air in my lungs to point out Judy's pun.

It's past four o'clock before Sam Wells finally leaves the house. Over the past hour my brain has been working at warp speed. Unfortunately, the pieces of the puzzle I've put together are embarrassingly lacking. Still, I have a hunch and want to follow up on it.

Sam Wells is your typical groupie. He tags along with Miller Stevens, probably gets some free pot and entertainment, but something tells me that the game is getting old. In the three times I've come across him in the past days, he's a shadow. Following Miller maybe, but not an active participant in anything the other man is doing. If I'm right, this hunch might pay off bigtime. If I'm wrong, well, I can't be any worse off than I am now, can I?

Standing inside the entry door to the enclosed staircase, my heart is beating loudly in my ears. I pat my jacket's pocket, feeling the small Glock 26 I added from my desk drawer. Called a "pocket Glock," this one is the perfect size for concealing, and its smallness makes it easy for me to use. Though I'm hoping that I won't have to.

Sam slouches out the door a minute later, stretching big as he glances down the street. I expect him to head to Miller's truck which is still parked outside my building, but instead he jogs across the road and into the liquor store nearby, adjusting his battered ball cap as he goes. I walk behind him, quietly, sticking to the shadowy area nearest the buildings. One eye on Sam's retreating back, I check the ground with the other. Stepping in a pile of dog poo is not going to make me a happy camper. I wait outside the liquor store, flipping my hood up over my face and wishing I had a cigarette to complete my look.

Instead, I pretend to text on my phone.

Minutes later he's emerging from the building, paper bag tucked under his arm. I take a deep breath as he glances around: my gun in my right hand in my jacket pocket, a pair of handcuffs in the other. I move closer, take a deep breath.

"Sam Wells, you're under arrest."

CHAPTER FIFTEEN

Impersonating a police officer is a crime. However, with Sam's record, I doubt I have much to worry about. I have to give the guy credit. Unlike Walter Hawk, Sam doesn't put up a fight, doesn't curse and call me names, doesn't even appear all that surprised. Maybe that was pot he was smoking in the house after all. His eyes are bloodshot, and his breath stinks as I hustle him off the sidewalk and into an alley near my building. I snap the handcuffs around his hands behind his back and he just shrugs and complies.

"I know you," Sam says, when I turn him around to face me. "I remember you from school. You're the one whose kid brother committed suicide."

"It wasn't suicide," I hiss in his ear and jerk him around so that I'm staring at his neck which is in need of a shave.

"Look, I'm not really a cop," I say, shoving him against the brick wall. Surprisingly, he still doesn't fight. "Alice hired me."

Sam exhales loudly. "I screwed up, I know. But maybe me and you can work out a deal. You can help me smooth things over with Alice, let her know that I'm working with you on a case against Miller Stevens. I can be your informant, you know? It's all gotten to be too much for me." He shakes his head mournfully. "The hard drugs, the prostitution. Hey, I've got my issues, but I'm a family man at heart." Sam rocks on his heels, takes another look across the road.

My wheels are turning.

"I can get more information for you; I help you out and you help me out. You've talked to Alice, and I know she must be missing me. And I miss her, the kids, too." Sam shakes his head. "Though not so much the kids. It's overwhelming, you know? Four kids, bam-bam-bam-bam, and now there's all this chaos and confusion. That's why I left—not permanent, just a little break. You know how it is, don't you? Got any kids?"

I just stare, not sure if I should laugh or muzzle him.

"Look, I know about what Miller's into, some of it anyway. If you let me go ..."

I suddenly find my voice.

"Do I appear to be an imbecile?" My voice is brittle. "There is no way I'm going to let you go. You're getting turned over to your wife who will hopefully kick your scrawny hiney for leaving her stranded. 'I just need a break," I say, in a whiny singsong. "And what is your wife supposed to do up there in the boondocks, stuck with four kids and no car?" I have an overwhelming urge to smack him across the head but refrain. An image of Alinah's smeary face earlier this afternoon runs through my mind.

"Did you hear what I said?" Sam's voice is more urgent but still low. "I can help you. I just need some time."

"And what kind of guarantee do I have that you're

telling the truth?" I hiss. "You don't seem like an especially trustworthy guy, Sam. All that drinking and drugging and deserting your family, stealing their only car. It makes a bad impression."

His head hangs for a moment, his hands relax fully in my grip. I keep my left hand pressed tightly on his bound wrists, the other hand holding my gun which is still in my pocket. I make sure to press it hard against the fabric so he knows that it's real. Sam, I notice, is still holding onto his bottle from the liquor store, wrapped neatly in brown paper.

"I know that. But this is different. I made a mistake, that's all."

I snort. "A mistake is doing something like spilling a soda or making a typo. You made a stupid decision. Let me tell you something, Mr. Wells." I lean in close, his chin barely above my own. "My therapist says that I have a lot of residual anger toward men. Don't make me take it out on you."

"I'm pretty sure your dad was set up."

This stops me in my tracks. For a moment no words will come out. Then I feel the gun imprinting itself on my palm and loosen my grip a little.

"What?"

"Your father is Jack Waters, right?"

Exhale.

Then, "What do you mean by set up? How? By who?"

Sam angles his body slightly so that he can look at me in the eyes. He's not a horrible looking guy. Chiseled cheekbones layered with a little scruff, straight Roman-looking nose, but acne has left scars, and his cheeks are

an angry red color over the facial hair. His face is
shadowed by the rim of the filthy ball cap.

"I know part of what happened that night. But if
you take me in now, you might never find out."

Circles start whirling in my mind like spinning
plates. Jack's face on one, Mama's on another, Alinah
and Miller and Doug and Sarjana.

"And if I let you go right now, who's to say that
you aren't going to run for the nearest border?"

Stupid, stupid, stupid. Don't even consider this, the
nagging voice in my head is yelling.

"I don't have nowhere to go. Don't have much
money either."

"There are ways around that."

"Maybe. But I'm not interested in finding them
out."

"Why not?"

Sam sighs, rolls his shoulders. "I know I messed up.
But I miss Alice. If I get the information that I need to
help you, then you can help me later. Help me patch
things up with Alice, make her see that I was helping
you out all along not that I just took off. Truth is, I don't
want to stay around here long-term anyway. Me and
Miller, we go way back, had a lot of good times
together, don't get me wrong. But he's headed down a
path I ain't comfortable following. And unless I get out
of here, out of this county, this state, it's going to be
hard to start over."

"So you're telling me that you want a fresh start.
Planning to leave Vermont."

Sam shrugs.

"Eventually. Is that a crime? Me and Alice have

been talking about Montana for a while now. Buy some land, get a trailer for the first few years till we can build a real place, you know. I'm ready for it. Gonna make a change for her and the kids, too. I already started alcohol counseling."

He says this last part proudly then glances at me as though looking for approval.

"So, just for fun, let's say that I was entertaining this thought. I let you go now and without any guarantee, you contact me with information, is that right? What about my payment?" No need for Sam to know that this is a freebie case. "You didn't show up with information, and I'm out my finder's fee."

Sam nods, slowly.

"If you give me five days, a week, I can get you information that might help your father. You scratch my back, I scratch yours, you know?"

"You touch me, and it's the last thing you do," I mutter. But I'm also thinking. Those plates keep spinning, and in the center of them, suddenly, is Sam's face. Then, "Two days. And what about a guarantee?" I ask.

Sam chews his lip for a minute then flexes his hand on the bottle of liquor. I remove my hand from the gun, take the bagged bottle from him and set it on the ground between us. I have a hunch and blurt out my thoughts before thinking better of it.

"Give me your hat."

Sam's eyes open wide. "Huh?"

"Your ball cap. I want that as part of the guarantee."

Sam stares. I look straight back at him.

"You must have had that thing, what, a decade?

Maybe more?" It's grubby and disgusting and looks like it's nearly at crustacean phase. "Whoever gave it to you must have been someone special."

Sam doesn't say anything, but I see gears and wheels turning behind his blue eyes.

"Fine," he says. "But can you release my hands first?"

I shake my head in a no-can-do way, then grimace as I look at the dirty brim and dirtier top of the ancient cap. It's impossible to tell what color it originally was. Flecks of paint and who knows what else litter its surface.

Yanking Sam back toward the corner nearest my car, I give him a shove in that direction. The sedan provides enough coverage that I doubt anyone across the street can see us. I reach through the open window and grab a plastic grocery bag. With the bag over my hand, I yank off Sam's hat then flip it inside. A move dog walkers do a hundred times a day when their precious pooches leave steaming piles on the sidewalks.

"You get this back in two days. Exactly two days from today, at exactly …" I glance at my watch, "five p.m. Got it?"

Sam starts to protest but I hold a hand up.

"Two days or no deal. I'm not waiting a week for information and my fee. I have bills to pay, too, you know."

He hesitates, thinking, then nods. I dig in my coat and extract a key for the cuffs and unlock his hands. A momentary pang of panic hits my gut. I deepen my voice and get in his face.

"If you so much as entertain a fleeting fantasy of

113

going out of town, I will know it. And then I will track you down, and you will ingest this," I shake the bag in his face. "I know where you're staying, and you might think that Miller is protection, but it would bring me no greater pleasure than to nail your hide to a tree."

Sam grunts. "Can I go now? Before they miss me ..."

"Five o'clock in two days. My office is upstairs," I point to the side drive of my building.

He returns to the house without any further comment. His hair, mashed into a ridge along his temple and forming a ring around his head, looks comical. I watch him go in, the door of the big house closing slowly behind him. What does he know about what happened with my father? Was Miller or my friendly neighbor Doug somehow involved in killing Sarjana and framing Jack?

Still sitting on my haunches, I chew a hangnail and then slap a hand to my forehead.

Dinner. My mother. Sophie.

Crap.

CHAPTER SIXTEEN

I'm eighteen minutes late pulling into the drive at my mother's house. It's a pretty place, a small, understated cottage on twenty acres. My mother has two dogs, thus the need for all the property, I guess. The house isn't nearly as spacious as the one we lived in as a family, but it has the same magazine-quality to it. The driveway and lawn are perfect looking, a wreath near the front door looks fresh, and the paint everywhere is smooth and unchipped. A small red shed stands to one side of the house; the other side boasts a white miniature version of the house itself. My mother's retreat. Why someone living alone needs a retreat, I'm not sure. Maybe it's to get away from her annoying dogs.

Ringing the doorbell, I smooth my hair down. I had exactly five minutes once I got home to give myself a sponge bath, apply deodorant and change into clean jeans. Cursing under my breath, I shift the bottle of liquor that I retrieved from Sam to my other hand.

"For heaven's sake, doll baby, you don't have to ring the bell! You're family." My mother, tall, blonde, beautiful, stands before me. She's wearing a pair of loose beige linen pants and a top with ruffles around the neck. Lillian is as breathtaking now as in photos I've seen of her in her pageant years. Her eyes have just a few crow's feet around them, her face a decade younger than her actual age. She reaches for the liquor, her other hand on my back, guiding me into the house.

"Come join us!" she says as I pull off my jacket. I leave it on a chair and follow her pointing finger to the living room. She follows behind me, tidying my jacket and hanging it on a hook in the entry way, smoothing the rug where my feet left it bunched and squirrely. I smile to myself. Though it's five-year-old behavior, I love to irritate her.

I pause outside the living room, trying to brace myself for my older sister. Sophie Mae Waters-Alexander sits in front of a fireplace covered with white pressed tin. The flames flicker and form a halo around her blonde head. *Typical.*

"Good of you to come, Tatum," Sophie says, not bothering to rise from the chaise lounge where she's perched. "You look ..." Pause. "...the same."

"Why thank you, Sophie." My voice is so saccharine I think I'm going to gag on its sweetness. "How's Buddy?"

Her back stiffens, shoulders tighten. A small crease forms between her perfect eyebrows.

"You know he doesn't go by that name. Why do you insist on being incendiary?"

"Incendiary? Me?" I hold my hand to my chest in mock dismay. "That's your job, Soph. You're the bigwig corporate lawyer. I'm just a little ole' country bumpkin, trailer trashin' my way through life. Yessum," I pause, wishing desperately I'd held onto the bottle of gin and simultaneously tickled at my mighty fine Appalachian accent. "I's just ..."

My mother walks into the room. Her face is crestfallen, as though I'd just kicked the dog or she'd found out I secretly enjoyed mistreating kittens. Lillian Rose does not appreciate the southern accent being mocked. Understandably.

I shut my fat mouth.

"Sorry," I mumble and fall into a straight-backed chair.

"God, Tayt," Sophie says, shaking her head in the way only a big sister can. "You can be so juvenile."

I bite my tongue. Hard.

"Would anyone like a canapé?" My mother comes closer, a white porcelain tray extended toward me. I thank her, take three and mash two into my mouth at once. My sister snorts in derision and holds a hand up to stop our mother.

"I'm on a strict life plan, Mother."

"Really? Are you giving up married men and divorces?"

The words literally spring from my food munching mouth with no consultation whatsoever with my brain.

"Tatum Rose!" My mother glares at me.

"Sorry," I say again. A few crumbs fall from my lips.

Sophie shoots me a withering glance but speaks only to Mama. "I told you about that detoxifying cleanse I tried, didn't I?" My mother nods and murmurs something I don't hear. "The next phase of it is called a synergetic life plan. It's all about changing the biochemical response of the body's ..."

I tune out, wonder again how exactly I ended up in this family, then rise from the uncomfortable chair and wander back into the kitchen. I don't really care for gin but pour myself a big tumbler full on ice and splash in some lemon juice I find in the fridge door. Two big swallows later, I'm pretty sure I could light a campfire with my tongue. My stomach burns, but then the heat turns to soft warmth and all my edges are a little less sharp. I take another swig, lean against the fridge.

"How's it going in there?"

The voice behind me is low, but I still nearly drop my glass in shock.

"Holy crap, are you trying to give me a heart attack, Buddy?"

Sigh.

"Please, don't call me that."

"Oh right. Sorry. Elliot."

There's another breath of silence between us, then I say, "I didn't know you were coming. No big mergers taking you out of the country?"

"Not this week."

My brother-in-law, Elliot Everston Alexander, is my sister's third husband. Fourth if you count the man she was living with between husband number one and two, but we don't usually. Elliot's in some sort of stock and brokerage trading that I absolutely can't understand. Not that I try very hard.

He's an alright guy, sort of dorky looking, tall and lanky with big glasses and hair that has a perpetual cowlick that Sophie hates. You'd think with all their money they could do something about that. But I guess my sister is just grateful that he has hair. He's ten years her senior, and his face has enough lines to prove it. In fact, he seems to have aged another ten since they've been married. Sophie's got a knack for that.

"What cases are you working on?" Elliot asks, then grimaces. "Sorry about your dad."

I nod. "Jack will be fine, I'm sure, as Jack always is. I've never seen my father get into a situation he can't weasel himself out of."

"But this is a murder case," Elliot reminds me, as though I'd forgotten.

Then, "Sorry, again. You know that," he says, taking a sip of seltzer.

"Geesh, Elliot. She can't see through walls. Can I pour you a real drink?"

My sister not only controls her own food and liquid intake like a hawk on speed, but her husbands' (past and present) as well.

Elliot swallows, eyes flitting to the bottle of gin and another of some expensive brandy my mother put near it.

"No, um, thanks anyway, but I'm fine."

We stand in uncomfortable silence for another moment. I, wishing he would morph into someone capable of riveting small talk, he, likely wishing I were the kind of sister-in-law that could explain the intricacies of my big sister's psyche. *No luck there, Buddy.*

I hear the *tick, tick, tick* of the clock in the entryway, and the stilted silence continues until my mother calls to me from the other room. I nod at Elliot and refill my drink, then think better of it and pour half into the sink. I have to drive home still. Hopefully soon.

"Tatum, listen to your sister's story about her latest win in the courtroom." My mother is fairly glowing as she looks in adoration at Sophie. Nausea sets in, and I'm thinking it's not the gin.

Sophie waves a well-manicured hand through the air.

"Oh, Mother. There's no need to bore Tatum with that. Tell me about what you're up to," Sophie says. "You know, at your ... work." She says the word as though it smells stinky.

Still, anything is better than talking about Jack.

I launch into a description of a few of my recent cases. Sophie wrinkles her nose in disgust and then loses interest halfway through my recount of Ezra's and my lake swim.

"Ugh, Tatum," Sophie gives a little shiver. "How can you stand to work with such, such ..." she searches for the right word, "... degenerates. Don't you find it depressing?" Before I can answer, she continues on.

"Remember when you were going to be someone, go to New York City? Broadway? But you never left this little Podunk town." She shakes her head, her pretty mouth downturned. "I don't know how you can stand it here. All these people you associate with."

An image of Winston comes to mind suddenly. My paranoid neighbor, frazzled, unkempt and often rude, is someone that falls into Sophie's *degenerate* category. But to me, he's a father figure. Someone who repairs my car, has helped me add on to my trailer, discovered I have a green thumb. Yes, he's crazy and frustrating and often shows up at the most inopportune moments, but underneath all that I know that he cares about me like the daughter he never had.

And suddenly my small home with all its coziness and the acres and acres of woods surrounding it and the solitude they impart are calling to me so loudly that my sister's voice is drowned out. I shake my head.

"I don't find it depressing. Everyone's got problems, Soph, even rich people. Maybe I get to see some peoples' problems up close and personal a little more than most, but that is sort of a gift. I guess you don't get that, but it is. It makes me grateful for all that I have."

I stand, pick up my glass and give her a little salute with it.

"Gotta go. Great seeing you."

Mama trails me to the door, protesting when I pull on my jacket and stuff my feet back into battered combat boots. I set my glass on a side table and she quickly picks it up, worried about water rings.

"I'll see you again soon," I say, kissing her on the cheek. "Elliot, have a safe trip home. It was nice chatting with you." I can't hear his murmured response but wave in that direction and back out of the door.

Cold, crisp October air greets me. The freshness of it is intoxicating, and I breathe deep and long. Throwing my head back, I see a hundred million stars and finally, finally, I can breathe again.

CHAPTER SEVENTEEN

The next morning dawns bright and clear. The sky is that beautiful, almost neon shade of blue that only happens in the fall. I've just finished my workout at the gym and am enjoying a good post-workout buzz, sipping coconut water on my way across the parking lot. There are a handful of other cars here, but the lot will be full in less than a half hour. Parents and senior citizens and more of us every-day-work-jerks cramming in quick sessions of cardio and sets of weights before heading off to kids, activities at the senior center and jobs, respectively. I toss my gym bag in the back and tuck shower-damp hair into a loose bun.

On my agenda this morning is an initial assessment and partial cleaning of a seasonal cabin near Hathaway Point Road. I wonder what sort of disaster looms before me. Taking on jobs sight unseen isn't part of my normal business model. But the pay will be good and steady since this is a property management gig and the hours flexible. The owners have gone back south for the cold months.

The car windows are cracked, and I hear the buzz of a small plane overhead, look up to see it dipping and diving and then floating among cotton ball clouds. The air is chilly on my face but smells so good I can't bear to close the windows back up. Wood smoke, heavy and rich, fills the air from houses I pass. The scent of decaying leaves and crumbly dirt, tired from another growing season, mixes in with the smoke.

Following the map along winding side roads I finally find the dirt road I'm looking for. It looks more like a gravel path. I follow it to the second drive on the left, a cottage set back from the road. Easing the car through the overgrown drive, I finally see the sight-unseen project that Repo Renew just took on.

Braced for the worst, I'm surprised to see how well-kept the exterior is. The small lawn is overgrown, and the windows facing the drive are dusty, but the paint is creamy yellow and unchipped. The wide screened-in porch is sturdy looking and perennial flowers flow from every conceivable place in the yard. Rusted buckets sport wild bunches of purple coneflower, holly hocks are tipping drunkenly near a tall wooden fence, daisies and black-eyed Susans and some sort of climbing wild roses run amok in an area that may have once been a proper English garden. The entire effect is wild and untamed. I love it.

Double checking the address, I verify I'm at the right house. Nothing makes an impression like trying to break and enter a home while someone is in it. This is the place, though.

I gather my cleaning supplies and a radio from the back and follow a twisty path to the front door. The smell of flowers, half-dead victims of a recent frost, mixes with the other fall scents.

The front door, painted periwinkle, squeaks when I open it. The inside smells musty, and all the rooms are dark. I flip the light switches and a few bare bulbs light up. It's small inside, with well-worn pine floorboards painted cream and heavy drapes covering the windows. Once these are pulled back, I look around the room again.

Amazing. It's like a little fairy cottage, complete with pressed tin ceilings and a fireplace made from recycled bottles and mortar. The windows are oversized in the small rooms, making them feel larger and more spacious. Light pours in, and I stand for a minute in the pool of sunshine, feeling it warm me from nose to toes.

I get to work, filling a bucket with hot, soapy water, pulling down the drapes to launder, washing, scrubbing and humming along to a station playing 90s grunge. Still, no matter how hard I scrub or how my arms burn with the effort, I can't get Sarjana out of my mind. Or Sam. Did I make a mistake? He'll likely screw me over, and then I'll be out not only two days' worth of time, but a chunk of self-esteem, too. *Stupid, Tatum. Really stupid. How can you be so naïve?*

I scrub harder, trying to silence the voice and reminding myself that every job comes with some amount of risk. If I worked in the stock market, I would have to take risks to succeed, right? Or if I were a lawyer like Sophie ... I shut that thought out before it goes any further. I'm not wasting an ounce of time thinking about Sophie.

I work until my arms are shaky, and my stomach growls. Then I lean back against a wall for a rest. I've just closed my eyes when I hear a cricket chirping loudly nearby. It takes a few seconds to realize it's my cell phone, alerting me of an incoming text message.

POTENTIAL LEAD ON A JOB FOR YOU. STILL
MAD AT ME?

C.J. is forever typing in all caps, which makes it
look like he's yelling in every one of his text messages. I
smile and type back.

No. I guess you have your uses. What's the job?
MEET ME FOR LUNCH?
OK. Where & when?
SNUFFYS. NOW? STARVING.
OK. C U in a bit.

Snuffy's is a greasy spoon on the corner of Lake
and Main Street. It's old and boasts a 50s inspired
interior. But unlike kitschy diners that have popped up in
recent years with a vintage vibe, Snuffy's is authentic.
The same red leatherette booths cradle the same chrome
tables that served patrons a generation ago. There's an
official soda fountain made of Vermont granite that
takes up an entire wall of the diner. The place still has
original black and white checkerboard floor, cracked and
stained in places. And Nanette, the owner's mother, a
fixture at the place, still sits on her high stool behind the
cash register, nodding at incoming patrons. She looks
like a tiny apple head doll, her face wrinkled and skin
brown.

"How're ya doin' today, sugar?" she asks me, her
voice surprisingly loud in such a small, bird-like body.
"Bring your appetite, I hope?" She maneuvers slowly off
the stool and hitches a thin arm around a menu, red, like
the booths.

"I did. How are you?"

She waves a thin hand through the air. "Can't

complain," she says, then proceeds to tell me about her arthritic back, problems with digestion and the recent hike in property taxes all the way to a back booth. She wears thick, white tights, like those that nurses used to wear, under a scratchy looking mulberry skirt. The tights sag and bag around her miniscule ankles. Bobby socks, with pompoms that bounce with every step, and crepe-soled shoes shuffle ahead of me.

"You meetin' anyone special today?" Nanette asks coyly, practically batting her lashes over the menus in her arms.

I smile. "Just C.J."

"Mmmmmm," she responds, licking her lips. "That's what I hoped you was going to say. That boy is one fine looking specimen." She grins and her tiny face looks surprisingly wolfish. "Don't let him get away." Her laugh starts out as a cackle and ends in a coughing fit.

I wait for her to stop and then say, "Don't worry, Nanette. It's not like that; C.J. and I are just friends. Besides," I lean closer and lower my voice to a whisper as the front doorbells clang, "I think he likes older women."

Her face lights up like Christmas, and she plops the menus on the table and pats at her chest area. "Really, now?" More patting, then some interior garment adjusting with gnarled fingers. "Well, I'll be." She takes our drink order and moves off to the front of the restaurant.

C.J. slides in a moment later, cheeks pink. I smile at him, point to the front area.

"Set up a hot date?"

"Shut up." C.J. buries his face in a menu and doesn't reappear until Nanette has come and taken our order. I would swear she did a little butt wiggle in his direction while departing, but it's hard to tell under that thick skirt.

"So," C.J. says, looking from the window to the mug of coffee he's stirring, "how are you holding up?"

I push the straw up and down in my soda, watching it bounce back every time with buoyancy. I'm envious of that straw. Lately I feel more like road kill—hit hard and plastered to the asphalt.

"Fine, I guess. Can't stop thinking about Jack."

C.J. nods but doesn't say anything.

"Judy's taken the case, though, and that makes me feel better. If anyone can get to the bottom of what's going on, it'll be her. Other than that, I'm just working my tail off, trying to keep up with the bills before they drown me."

"You'll never drown. You know that, don't you? I've told you before—"

I wave away the rest of his sentence. "I appreciate your offer to help, but I'm fine. I can manage on my own."

"You've made that perfectly clear on many levels."

Now it's my turn to blush, but my skin isn't fair like my dining companion. Instead, I wiggle uncomfortably in my seat.

We sit in silence another uncomfortable moment, me perusing the placemat with interest, C.J.'s gaze perusing my face.

Then he asks, "Up for another job?"

It never rains but it pours.

"Maybe. What do you have?" I ask, rearranging my cutlery on the pristine paper napkin. I exhale a breath I didn't know I was holding, grateful to be back on solid professional ground.

C.J. shifts on his side of the booth, the material squeaking in protest as he rearranges his tall frame. He waits to take a sip of his coffee, makes a face and stirs in two more creamers simultaneously.

"Does this woman bake the joe or what?"

"Maybe you can tell her just how you like it when you're at her place." I smile sweetly.

He frowns at me but continues.

"I've heard about a missing woman, Patty Commo. Her grandmother knows my aunt, you know Aunt Amanda, the hairdresser? Anyway, you know how the grapevine around here is. The grandmother hasn't called it in to the barracks yet, or the local PD as far as I know. So, it would be a good time for you to offer your services. The old woman's worried. The case might be a dud, though. Sometimes people are just tired of life and skip town to go on a little road trip or something."

I think of Sam Wells and feel my gut tighten.

"It might be. What's her story, the woman who is missing?" I take another sip of soda, the fizziness making my eyes tear for a second.

"She's not a shiny penny or anything; I did a little digging for you. Petty larceny and possible embezzlement at her last place of employment, Stevens' Auto Shop. No previous violent acts on her record."

I bolt upright in my seat at the mention of the auto shop owned by Miller Stevens. C.J. glances at me weirdly, and I try to recreate my earlier slouch. This job has suddenly gotten a lot more interesting.

"So, why does the grandmother think it's a big deal? The woman is of age, isn't she?"

"Late thirties. Grandma says Patty stops to see her every day, makes sure the old lady has set her meds up correctly, runs her errands, that type of thing. She told Amanda that if Patty didn't show up, then something is wrong. She would have called. Grandma doesn't drive, and it's unclear where her daughter, Patty's mother, is. Guess the two don't get along."

I nod. "Anything else on her record? Patty's, I mean, not Grandma's."

C.J. shrugs. "Small stuff. Couple of tickets for speeding, one for disturbing the peace and another for public drunkenness. But that last charge was during the Grateful Dead concert in '95. Who wasn't drunk then?"

I nod. I wasn't, but then not everyone was dealing with a brother who was an addict. I block the image of Max out of my head and focus on C.J instead.

"It's hard to remember you that way," I say now. "Instead of a lawman, you were the law breaker." It's the perfect opportunity to reminisce, to start my next sentence with, *"Remember the time ..."* But I don't want to remember. And C.J. doesn't want to forget.

He shrugs, offers a slow grin. "Got respectable. What can I say? It was to impress you, you know. When you got back from college, I gave you a shock. Admit it." His smile grows bigger. I'm the one to shift in my seat now, and it squeaks in protest.

"Unfortunately, not as impressed as I'd hoped." His smile fades, and he laces his fingers under his chin, his cornflower eyes studying me again.

I clear my throat. This water is way too familiar, and I'm not a good swimmer.

"Grandma have any idea where Patty's gone?"

He looks out the window then shakes his head.

"Business as usual, huh?" C.J. sighs. Then, "Are you ever going to forgive me? It was a long time ago, and it was a stupid mistake."

I press my lips together; my stomach twists.

"You know the deal, C.J."

And he does. We can be friends as long as he doesn't try to make it into anything else. What it used to be.

"Right. The deal."

We stop talking when a guy wearing a grease-stained apron stops by our table, arms laden with plates.

"Snuffy, how're you doing?" C.J. asks the long-haired man in his mid-forties, Nanette's son. The thin gene apparently runs rampant in their family. His skinny arms stick out like plucked chicken wings as he lowers the diner plates to our table.

"Hey, man. Good to see you. Doing good." He nods to me, round, wire-rimmed glasses bobbing up and down on a nose that's hawkish and shiny. Speaking of the Grateful Dead, Snuffy is a poster child for the hippy band.

"Get you anything else?" he asks, surveying the table.

C.J. has his mouth so full of burger that all he can manage is a, *"mmmnooooommmm."*

"I think we're all set," I say. Snuffy nods and smiles, then meanders back toward the kitchen door.

When he's done chewing, C.J. says, "Patty has

family out of state, according to Amanda via Granny. Some in New York and more down toward Massachusetts. No idea if she'd go to them, but it might be a good place to start looking."

I pull out a notebook and pen and get more details over my greasy spoon special.

CHAPTER EIGHTEEN

It's past two o'clock when we re-emerge into the now blinding afternoon sun. C.J. pulls on his aviator glasses.

"Do they hand those things out at the academy? I've always wondered."

He shakes his head. "Nope. I just know how good they make me look."

I snort, start walking slowly down Lake Street where I'd wedged the car into a parking spot. C.J. trails behind, checking his cell, but soon his long strides catch up with me. He looks over my car.

"When are you going to admit defeat?" His brow is furrowed as he surveys the ancient sedan.

"Ugh, you and Ezra. What is it with my car? This vehicle is trustworthy, sweet, and loyal. It's a trait that not many men have these days, yet you both want me to toss the car aside like rubbish."

"That's because it *is* rubbish, not to mention completely unsafe for you to be driving, living and working where you do. On this one, small matter, Ezra and I agree."

I shake my head.

"That's just it. It's exactly the kind of car that I

need for where I work and live. There's no danger of theft, it blends in, and when parts fall off, no one even notices the additional debris."

CJ shakes his head. "What are you doing the rest of today?"

I think about my answer. I should probably go back to the cottage and keep cleaning, but my arms and legs tell me otherwise.

"Go have a chat with Patty's grandmother, I guess. See what I can find out about her friends, the family that you mentioned."

"You're welcome," C.J. says. I reach and grab his forearm.

"Yes, thank you. I'm sorry, I forgot to tell you earlier. Too distracted by your flirtations with Nanette, I guess." I smile.

I imagine his eyes rolling behind the mirrored shades but he smiles. It's slow and lazy, and I feel something in my gut that I don't want to feel. I pull my hand back and open the driver's door. A loud squawk covers up his words.

"What?" I ask.

"I said, any time, Tayt. You know that, right?" His eyebrows lift above the dark glasses, and I picture the crinkles around his blue eyes.

"Right," I say and hop in. "Thanks again."

I wave and pull my seatbelt on, check over my shoulder and even use my signal before pulling out in traffic. Feeling C.J.'s eyes following my tail lights always makes me a better driver, at least for a block or two.

It takes that long for me to get my breathing back to

normal. I've never been one of those women who can be "just friends" with an ex, so this is a first-time thing for me. I wish for a minute that Sophie was a nice sister, one that I could share secrets with or ask embarrassing questions of. Cause there's a question burning in my brain: Is it normal to still have feelings for someone that you don't want to have feelings for ever again?

Once I've rounded the corner and passed over the railroad tracks on Oak Street, I add more weight to the gas pedal. My cell rings, and I recognize Judy's mobile. I pull over near a T-ball field and answer.

"Got some word on the missing woman," Judy says.

"Really?" My heartbeat speeds up, and I hold the phone closer to my ear, trying to drown out the sound of a delivery truck backing up nearby.

"Do you remember reading about a prostitution ring that was busted in the Burlington area a few years back?"

Tightness pulls my chest closed. I can barely nod an affirmative, then realize stupidly that my former mentor can't see me. She continues on anyway.

"Well, she was apparently one of the women arrested. It was," Judy is silent a moment, and I picture her adjusting the red-framed reading glasses, "a sex trafficking ring. There were six women in all, working out of a massage parlor. A front for what I'm sure was a very profitable business venture. Their pimps were a fifty-year-old guy and his son, both residents of the area. Creeps." Judy swears under her breath then heaves a big sigh.

"I remember hearing about it. Vaguely. I don't remember many of the details." My voice is shaky, but if

Judy notices, she doesn't say anything.

"It was ugly, the two guys served a minimum amount of time and went along their merry way. The women, all of them here illegally, were jailed and then were supposed to be deported to their country of origin. I'm not sure how your friend's cousin found her way up to St. Albans, but she must have slipped through the cracks somehow."

"This was how many years ago?"

Judy is quiet for a minute, then I hear her reading under her breath. "Ah, here. The article is dated three years ago."

"My God. Sarjana couldn't be more than eighteen now. Have been," I correct myself. Then, "How does a fifteen year old girl from Malaysia end up a prostitute in the U.S.? In Vermont of all places?"

Judy snorts.

"What do you know about sex trafficking?" she asks.

"Not much. Just what I've heard in the news. That it's mostly overseas. India, Asia?"

"Do some research. You'll learn a lot. My oldest niece is involved with an organization that works against it. Pretty eye-opening. Sickening, too."

Her voice is muffled for a moment as she speaks to someone else in the room. "Sorry, I have to run. Literally," she says. "Take care, and I'll keep you posted. Oh, and I found out that the victim's body will be returned to Malaysia within the next couple of days. Apparently a great aunt or someone has claimed it."

My stomach is churning, acidic and hot as I lean back in the seat and end the call after thanking Judy for the information. *There were scratches on my arms.* I picture Jack, staring at the table in the visiting room. *Mud on my boots, on my pant legs ... I found women's clothes all balled up in the corner, behind the couch.*

Alinah's face appears again in my mind, mottled and swollen.

I jam the stick shift into drive and pull out too hard and fast from the parking area. Gravel sprays out and pings off a yield sign nearby, and I nearly hit a skinny white cat that chooses that moment to race across the street. Slamming on the brakes, the seatbelt snaps hard against my chest and I lose my breath.

Do some research, Judy said.

I plan to.

An hour and a half later, sweat pours from my face. I've been working the bag at the gym for a good thirty minutes. One workout a day is my limit. Usually. But sometimes if I need to blow off some steam, take out some frustration or maul something without being arrested, I make exceptions. There are people who eat too much ice cream or drink until they're stupid. I hit things. If my arms and legs felt rubbery after all the scrubbing this morning, now they resemble goo. My heart is pounding hard and fast in my chest which is heaving under the effort of keeping up with my fists and feet.

"Looking good, Tatum," a man's voice calls out. I glance over quickly, see the owner, Jake, and give a quick wave.

"Leave some of the bag intact for other people," he says with a laugh.

I grimace and throw another series of punches, quick and hard. The shock of each one reverberates up my arms and into my chest, shaking my ribcage, but I want to feel more of it. Lowering my head, I grunt and hit the bag again and again. I want my body to hurt so that I can't think about anything else. Want to wipe out the events of the last few days with sweat and spent muscles and aching limbs.

I picture Miller Stevens' stupid face and deliver a roundhouse kick so hard that I half expect it to shatter my femur. I saw a photo of the pimps/spa owners in Burlington and envision their faces as I plant a series of jabs and uppercuts so fast that the bag barely has time to bounce in between punches. Every hit on the bag loosens more images of what I've just seen and read on the computer, "doing my research" as Judy suggested.

The faces of young women and children move in and out of my thoughts like ghosts. Statistics bounce around my head like ping pong balls. Sex trafficking is the second largest industry in the world, second only to drugs. Millions of women and kids are kidnapped, tricked or forced into prostitution, not only abroad but right here in the good ole' US of A. I read some of the stories, firsthand accounts of the brutality that these women and children endured. Many of them will never tell their stories, killed by their pimps, by AIDS or by their own hand as they stare into hopeless futures.

I smash both hands into the bag with a low growl. One of the two men sparring in the ring nearest me glances my way. His partner takes the opportunity to land a quick foot to his solar plexus, and he lets out a loud grunt.

Clutching the bag, I wrap both arms around it. This time it's to keep me upright. Sobs, deep and slow, wrack my body. The events from the last few days mix with the images I've just seen and the burning anger in my gut. Bending my head low so no one will see, I swipe at my eyes with my hand wraps, give a final, half-hearted kick to the bag and head for the locker room.

CHAPTER NINETEEN

Patty Commo lives in a trailer park off of Route 78 in Highgate. I've just left her grandmother's house and have Patty's address, a photo, and some other notes tucked into my bag.

The trailer park is neat and tidy, small strips of lawn blocking off equal rectangles between mobile homes. One sports a few faded flamingos tipping over near a spent garden. Another, a wishing well painted dark gray and made from what looks like reclaimed wood pallets. Patty's trailer is the second from the last on the left and is completely bare of personality, an older brown model that sports concrete steps and cream curtains drawn in every window.

I get out of the car slowly, not because I'm feeling cautious, but because after the gym I can barely move. Every muscle in my body is begging me for a hot bath and bed. I ignore their pleas and force myself gingerly up the front steps.

Dusk is just setting, and I hear the low hoot of an owl in a grove of trees nearby. The call, *who-cooks-for-you-who-cooks-for-you-all* echoes around the park. I mount the steps slowly and knock. A curtain nearest the door moves slightly, but the light over the front porch remains off. Dried bug remains stain the bulb's surface. The front door doesn't budge. I open the flimsy aluminum storm door and wedge myself between it and the door frame, knock again, louder. No movement. I wait a minute, then three, then sigh. I don't have time for this crap tonight, and this pain in the hiney is standing between me and a hot bath.

"Hello? Ms. Commo, I know you're in there. Can you please open the door?"

No response.

"My name is Tayt Waters. I'm from T.R. Waters Security. I just have a couple of questions for you."

Questions like, "Should I kick your butt before or after you see your grandmother and assure her you're not dead?"

I bang again, loudly enough that the neighboring trailer owner pokes a head around a paisley curtain and presses her nose against the glass. I wave halfheartedly, smile and hope I look un-menacing.

"Hello?" I call out again. But of course, there is no response. I consider the possibilities. Option A: Patty Commo is stupid enough to be hiding out in her own trailer and refusing to open the door. Option B: Someone else is staying at Patty's trailer and not about to open the door to a stranger. Option C is interrupted when the neighbor woman appears at my arm.

"Looking for Patty, honey?" A twist tie dangles from the corner of her mouth. Her lipstick is orangish and nearly glows in the fading light. She's small and thin with a pot belly and an old-fashioned smock top, her tiny feet pushed into Keds that have seen better days.

"Good evening, Ma'am," I say. "Yes, I'm looking

for Patty Commo. Have you seen her around?"

She sighs, hand fishing in the smock top. She pulls out a blister pack of dissolvable vitamin C tablets and pops four in her mouth.

"Sorry, I'd offer you one, but these puppies are so dang expensive now, I've weaned myself back to only one a day." One blister pack? Or one box full? I shake my head.

"No problem." Then, "Do you happen to know where she is?"

The woman frowns, puts a wrinkled hand to her chest, then belches. The smell of garlic overpowers me, and I unconsciously take a step back.

"Whew. Sorry about that. Garlic don't agree with my system, but I can't stay away from it. Baked, boiled, stewed, sprinkled, I eat it any which way. It's delicious and an excellent anti-inflammatory, too. I take that and my pills," she pats her pocket, "and I'm healthy as a horse." She waves a hand through the air as though to push away the noxious odor. "Haven't been sick in six years." She smiles, nods her head.

I jerk my head toward the brown trailer. "Patty?"

"Oh, she's gone, honey. Left two days ago, I think it was? Or maybe yesterday. The days all sort of blur together once you retire. Got herself in some trouble with the law's what I heard. You live this close to your neighbors, and you'll see firsthand how fast word spreads." She waves an all-encompassing arm around the mobile homes.

A headache is forming between my eyes and around the outer edges of my skull.

"Any idea who's in her house?" I whisper loudly,

pointing at the trailer behind me.

"Huh?" The woman's head snaps toward the place, then her finger follows. "Her house?"

I nod. *Breathe, Tayt, breathe.* Feeling proud, I manage to say without an ounce of sarcasm, "Yes."

The woman shakes her head.

"That's not Patty's house. She lives across the way, number seven-oh-six. Blue place with a bunch of lilac bushes out front."

I look at the note in my hand, then from the woman to the front door of the brown trailer. Faded numbers clearly indicate that this is number nine-oh-six. *I'm such an idiot.*

"My mistake," I say, stuffing the paper into my pocket and stepping backward. "It's been a long freaking day, and I think I'm going to call it quits before I do anything else stupid."

"Too late," says the woman, pointing her finger toward my foot.

The smell of dog crap wafts gently upward.

At twenty-five past nine the next morning, I'm standing on the front porch of Alinah's, two cups of coffee in hand. She answers my knock after a few minutes, looking disheveled and sleepy.

"Hi," I smile through the screen door. "Coffee?"

She studies me for a moment, face expressionless, then looks over her shoulder.

"No good time."

"We can sit in the park, just for a few minutes." I coax with the paper cup held near the door, hoping the smell will entice her if my smile doesn't. She chews her bottom lip, checks the room behind her again, then nods.

"You wait one minute?"

I smile bigger. "Sure."

She reappears on the porch moments later, stuffing her arms into a light jacket, and we duck off the steps and follow a narrow alley, the back way to a small playground on a nearby street. There are three park benches grouped under towering elm and maple trees, and we choose the one in the sunniest spot. Alinah thanks me for the cup as I hand it to her but doesn't sip. Her long brown fingers hold it gently while she looks up into the tops of the red and yellow trees.

"Sar is dead." She says the words without emotion, but I see a small vein throb just over her right temple.

"I know, and I'm so sorry."

She turns to me.

"How you know?"

"I know the person accused of her ..." my voice stumbles but then rights itself, "of her murder. He didn't do it." I rush the words. "But somehow he's involved with what happened. I'm trying to figure out how so that we can catch the real killer."

"Why?" Her voice trembles. At first I think she's asking why are we trying to find the killer, but then she continues. "Why someone kill Sar? She sweet girl, good girl. Why ..." Her voice breaks then, and she sets the coffee on the ground near her feet, hands cover her face. Her sobs are soundless, but teardrops dampen her jeans. I put a hand tentatively on her back, rub in a little circular motion. My mother used to do this when I was small, and I hope it comforts Alinah as much as it used to me. Of course, I was being comforted for things like scratched knees and mean boys on the playground, not a murdered cousin.

We sit in silence for a few minutes, Alinah crying and me rubbing circles on her back and murmuring unhelpful platitudes.

"I'm going to find who did this, Alinah, I promise. I have a friend who's a PI, a private investigator. We'll figure this out. Whoever did it will be arrested."

Alinah nods once, then wipes her face on the sleeve of her jacket. She leans back on the bench, eyes closed. The sun makes her dark hair glow with reddish highlights and her skin nearly translucent.

"Can you tell me anything about that night?" I ask.

She picks up the cup again, takes a small sip then leans back, one long leg crossed over the other. Her eyes are red-rimmed, her lips tremble.

She shakes her head and then speaks. "I not know. Not much. Doug, our ... " her voice breaks off and she glances toward the big, white house. "Doug tell me she left late that night. Then she not come back."

"But where did she go—she doesn't drive, does she?"

"Sar no drive."

"What about a taxi?" I ask then feel like smacking my hand against my forehead. *Idiot.* I should have thought to call the local cab companies. I make a note to do that as soon as I get back to the office. But then Alinah tells me that no, they've never ridden in a taxi before.

"Maybe she go in car with someone," Alinah says. "Maybe truck."

The fact that she said, "truck" makes my heart skip

a beat. Miller Stevens has a truck, a big, hulking black one.

I nod. "Any idea who?"

She shakes her head.

I think about what I saw on the internet, the photos and statistics. How do I broach this subject without causing a divide between Alinah and me? You can't just blurt out a question like, "Are you a victim of sex trafficking?" My mind spins for a few minutes, and we sit in silence. In the end, Alinah breaks it and her words surprise me.

"You my friend, Tayt," she says. "You only friend here. I have secret. I tell you, you keep it, right?" I nod without thinking of the consequences.

Alinah takes a heavy, shoulder shuddering breath.

"I not here OK, you know?" She pauses, searching for words. "I no here legally. Sar and me—from Malaysia—not from here."

She shivers, glances again toward the house. Her fingers are so tight on the paper cup of coffee that they're white-tipped.

"We stolen here," she says.

"Stolen? Do you mean, taken—abducted?"

She frowns then nods.

"Taken."

"When?"

"Me five years pass. Sar, just maybe three year. She younger. We no come together."

There is a knot the size of a football in my gut, twisting.

"But you are family? Cousins, right?"

She shakes her head again.

"No related. I call cousin, but she like sister to me." Her voice breaks again, and she sets the cup on the bench near her hip, holds a hand to her mouth as though trying to push the emotion back in.

"Alinah," I speak slowly, place a hand on top of the one resting on the bench near the coffee. "Are you a prisoner? Is Doug," I pause, "is Doug keeping you?"

She nods, tears forming again on her cheeks.

"I no go home. Doug keep me here to work. They told me one year to pay my way, but then take my papers, my ..." she searches for a word, "my passport papers. I no have money, no have ID. Doug, he second man I work for here. He tell me 'one more year, one more year' but I still work."

I swallow. My throat is dry, the roof of my mouth feels like paste.

"What does he make you do, for work?" My heartbeat drums in my ears, my face, hot.

Her words are so quiet, so small, I nearly miss them completely. A wind drives dry leaves against our legs, her voice as scratchy as they sound tumbling on the ground.

"I make men happy. Give massage, do what they want."

I suspected this, knew it deep down. But to hear the words makes me nauseous just the same.

"Alinah?" A man's voice splits the quiet of the park. Alinah jumps as though a shock hit her system. Her coffee spills over the bench and the ground beneath. Doug stands on the edge of the property, looking toward us, a scowl on his face.

CHAPTER TWENTY

Alinah is on her feet, hands fluttering over her hair, her face. She shoves tangled strands away from her face, wipes her eyes again.

"I go now," she says. Her voice is shaking.

"Wait," I say, hand in my left pocket. I glance back toward the house, see Doug checking out a pretty blonde pushing a baby carriage. Pulling out a new pre-paid cell phone, I press it into Alinah's palm. "I bought this for you, just in case. Call me. I'm going to help you. My number is programmed in, along with dispatch at the police station and the women's abuse shelter. Call me, please, anytime."

She shoves the small phone into the pocket of her jacket and hurries away. I don't trust myself to look at Doug again, sure he'll see rage written all over my face. Instead, I sit on a swing facing the other direction and look out toward the strip of brown and green grass separating the park from the immigration building parking lot.

The swing gives a loud squeak with every push. The toes of my boots burrow into the sand and loose gravel under my feet. The playground reminds me of school days: robin's egg blue skies and laughter, cheeks

147

reddened by chilly wind and lilac-colored woolen mittens. But the only laughter I hear is the echo of childhood ghosts. Even the sun disappears behind gray clouds, as though it can't bear Alinah's story either.

My cell phone rings, the noise cutting through the gentle breeze and squeaking of the swing so loudly that I jump. I fish in my pocket and answer before it goes to voicemail.

"Tatum?" My mother's voice is soft as butter, but something hard and sharp lies beneath the surface.

"How are you, Mama?"

"I've been better, sugar. I need a ride, please. If you can come now, I'd be most grateful."

My mother's asking is actually more like telling. I squirm in the swing's seat.

"Now?"

"Yes, please, if you would."

"Where to?"

"The county jail. I need to speak to your father."

I groan internally. Just what I need.

"Well, I could call you a cab, Mama. I'm actually just going into my office." I stand and start walking in that direction. It's not a lie if I'm in the process, right?"

"No. Thank you, Tatum, but I need you to take me. I won't be long. I'll be expecting you in ten minutes."

She hangs up before I can say anything else. I stare disbelieving at the phone for a few long seconds. Did my mother really just hang up on me? My cultured, polite, lovely mother?

Twelve minutes later—I drove past the private road and back twice just to make sure I wasn't within the ten minute timeframe—I pull into my mother's driveway. She appears seconds later, dressed in silky looking pants, a pumpkin-colored jacket belted around her waist. Her blond hair is short and wavy over high cheekbones, topped with a pair of designer sunglasses. Even now, after all these years, sometimes her beauty takes my breath away. I'm suddenly conscious of my own grubby appearance. Jeans that have been worn three times without washing, a flannel shirt that I found on the floor of my closet and my favorite pair of Doc Martins. I smooth the shirt down, button my army green jacket over it and re-wind the scarf around my neck.

"Darling, thanks for the ride," my mother says climbing into the car's interior. I move the plastic bin of cleaning supplies to the back seat from the passenger's side floor.

"Sorry," I say, waving a hand around the car. "My Jag is in the shop."

Mama smiles, nods absently and stares out the window. Trees and underbrush blur past, and we turn onto Route 7 following the winding road into St. Albans. We don't speak for several minutes, but when we do it's her voice that interrupts the silence.

"Tatum, I want you to come in with me."

I nod.

"Sure."

"I want you to talk some sense into your father. He's adamant that he won't plead guilty, but our attorney feels that his sentence will be significantly reduced if he does. The evidence gathered so far is completely damaging. I need you to convince him. He'll listen to you."

My gut twists. I sit in silence another moment, listening to the loud hum of the car's tires against the pavement.

"I appreciate your confidence in me, Mama, but I can't do that."

"Of course you can, sugar!" My mother's voice is still honey-sweet, but that dark undertone is still there. "You can and you must. Your father is in a very bad place, Tatum, and he's not making wise decisions right now."

"I know about the place Jack is in, Mama. I've been to see him. I've seen his ..." I break off for a moment, thinking about the sad, scared face and sagging shoulders, "his response to the situation. But pleading guilty for a crime he didn't commit? I can't try to talk him into that. Not that he'd listen to me anyway."

I glance in her direction. Her mouth is pulled into a tight line. The fact that I'm defending my father against Mama is irony that isn't lost on me.

We don't speak again until entering the jail. After the guard signs us in, we walk back to the visiting room. This time the temperature is greenhouse hot, and I have to remove my jacket immediately. My mother frowns at my flannel shirt but says nothing.

Moments later, Jack is led into the room. He's wearing an orange prison jumper with a number stamped in black over his left breast. His eyes are red-rimmed, his skin ashy gray. He's sporting a cut over his left eye that burrows into the brow.

"My God," Mama breathes. "Look at you."

I clear my throat. Her voice is full of sadness, and for one horrible minute I think they're both going to start crying.

"You look like crap, Jack," I say. My mother shoots me a withering glance then looks back toward my father.

My father's hands are trembling, but he smiles at my words, then sits slowly, creakily down in the folding chair on his side of the table.

"I've been better." His voice is gravelly, unused. I nod to the guard, Ben, I think his name is. He exits the room but leaves the door open.

"Jack," my mother's voice is still shaky. "We need to discuss your plea. Mr. Hendricks feels ..."

My father raises his hand, head bowed. "Lillian, I know what you're going to say. I heard you on the phone last night. But I can't. I can't plead guilty to something I didn't do, don't remember doing."

"There's physical evidence, Jack!" My mother's voice has lost a little of its honeyed edge. "There is evidence linking you to this ... this ..." She searches for words then glances to the corner of the room, as though expecting the rest of her sentence to appear from stage right. "To the crime," she finally says.

"I know that, Lily." My father's voice is slow and low. I lean forward to hear. "But I know that I didn't do this. I couldn't have. I was unconscious for pity's sake!"

There are two minutes of awkward silence as each of us stares at various uninteresting objects in the room. My mother becomes fascinated in a light switch on the far wall, my father at the table top in front of him. I study my boots.

"I know who the woman was," I say finally. "She lived in the apartment building across the street from my office. Her name was Sarjana." My father's head snaps up as though I've slapped him.

"Sarjana," He repeats softly. Then, "What do you know about her?"

I swallow, eyes tracing the red laces of my boots with renewed interest.

"She was eighteen. From Malaysia originally."

My mother's hands are over her mouth. At the mention of Sarjana's age, I heard a gasp from her direction. Tears are leaking out over the dam her fingers have made.

"Poor, poor baby. Just a baby," she murmurs. My father shifts uncomfortably in his seat.

"My God." Jack says the words like a prayer. "Eighteen years old. That's how old ..." And we can all finish his unsaid sentence if we wanted. That's how old Max was when he died.

My father is silent a long while, rubbing his hands together then over his face. Finally, sighing, he says, "I haven't heard much from Judy, have you?"

I nod, finally feel like I can exhale.

"She's doing what she can. Got a partial, unofficial report from the coroner's office from a connection there and trying to put pieces together. She said Sar ... the woman's body will be sent back home to family, given a proper burial there."

My father nods; my mother digs in her handbag and pulls out a small packet of tissues then delicately smooths wetness from her face.

"I've connected with Alinah, a friend of Sarjana's. I was just talking to her this morning, actually. The girls are involved in a sex trafficking ring." I hold up a hand as my mother gasps. "I think I might be able to find out more about what happened that night, I just need a little time. I also have another," I pause thinking of a word to describe Sam Wells that doesn't make him sound as sketchy as he is, "connection. Between Alinah and Sam, we'll have a better idea—."

"But that's still no reason to put off talking to Mr. Hendricks, Jack." My mother interrupts in a voice that has turned squishy. She looks at him, eyes pleading. "Please. Just listen to him, and do what he says. Your life is at stake here."

My father looks from me to my mother, then back. He addresses his next sentences to me, but I know they're intended more for her.

"I can't do it. I have to find out what happened that night. I need to know, or I'll never have any semblance of peace. I appreciate your concern, Lillian, but I have to do what I feel is right and best."

A mixture of emotions runs through my body. Pity, yes, but not enough to cover the anger, deep and dark and old. Like a crustacean firmly embedded, the rage is always with me.

"Like you did all those years ago?" I say. "Like you did with Max?" The words are so bitter I half expect them to singe my tongue.

My father's head reels as though I've hit him physically. I hear a sharp intake of breath from my mother whose hand suddenly flies toward her mouth.

"Tatum," she says. "Please don't."

This conversation is far too familiar. I stand up and look at my father. He has two bright red patches over each cheekbone. His hair is greasy, and he looks more disheveled than I've ever seen him. But I recognize the look in his eyes. Anger. Fury, maybe. But something else, something that I haven't seen before. Regret, I think.

And he should feel regretful. Jack, the great career man; the flirt; the man who in the early days could make Mama laugh like no one else. And later the man who broke both her and his kids' hearts when he decided another woman and family were more his style. Handsome and selfish Jack, responsible for my brother's death.

CHAPTER TWENTY-ONE

"I can't believe you, Tatum Rose," my mother says as we climb back into the car. "Can't you show your father a little mercy? A bit of forgiveness?"

My response? A snort. Not very mature, I'll admit, but heat has climbed up from my gut, threatens to overwhelm me.

"What happened with your brother ..." Mama begins, but I hold up a hand to stop the flow of words. Words that I've heard a zillion times and which will be no more comforting or meaningful than the first.

"Please, Mama, I don't want to get into this again."

"You don't want to get into it?" My mother's voice is loud in the enclosed space, and I glance her way. Now it's her turn to sport reddened cheeks, though it only makes her even more beautiful somehow. "Jack is your father, Tatum. You need to show some respect."

"And trying to find out what happened, fix whatever it is that he did, isn't doing that? Mama, I'm trying to start a business here, and I've already got one in the works. Do you know how hard it is to balance everything? And on top of that I get this," I wave my hand toward the jail, "dumped in my lap. I haven't seen Jack in years, and I'm trying my best to be his knight in shining armor. But please, don't tell me that I'm being disrespectful. He doesn't deserve my respect or yours or Sophie's. And yet I'm helping him, despite that. God knows why, but I am."

I crank the engine, and we retrace our path to her house in silence. Mama stares out the window, head leaning back on the sagging headrest. The heat in my belly grows cooler the more miles I drive, but it's not gone. It never is. I try and fail to push away images from all those years ago. Max, the beautiful artist, tanned skin growing pale, already thin frame growing gaunt, eyes hollow. His paintings had turned from vibrant and whimsical to dark and oppressive, haunting.

Opiate addiction is more prevalent in Franklin County than ever before. Some blame the poor socioeconomics, others an influx of drug dealers who use the rural community as a stopover, pushing drugs from New York City upwards to Montreal and other outlying areas in Canada. Max was just one more addict.

My cell phone rings, interrupting my thoughts, and I welcome it.

"Tayt. Judy."

My mentor sounds out of breath. This is normal. She's likely training for an upcoming long-distance marathon or uber crazy bike race.

"Found something interesting." *Huff, puff.* "Eye witness places a big pickup leaving your father's place," *Huff, puff.* "In the wee hours the night of the murder. Out walking his dog." *Huff, puff.*

"That's awesome," I say. "Any chance he nabbed the license plate number?"

Huff, puff.

"Nope. But he said it was loud, probably had a

Hemi and definitely had two of those tall chrome exhaust stacks coming off the back." *Huff, puff.*

My fingers are clenching the phone so tightly I'm amazed it doesn't begin to conform to the shape of my fingertips.

Miller.

"I think I know the owner of that truck," I say, voice surprisingly normal. "Miller Stevens. A local-yocal. Lives down on Maquam Shore." I clear my throat. "I've been talking with one of his buddies. He's a possible informant, but I need another day for information."

I hear Judy's big sigh following yet another gasp for air.

"You're not supposed to be working this case, Tayt. You know the laws and the requirements of being a PI. If you get caught—"

"I know, but it's my father."

"The judicial system doesn't care about that. Not even a little bit so don't lie to yourself. *Huff, puff.* Get tangled up in the red tape and you could lose both of your businesses."

There are days when this feels more like a blessing than a curse, but I understand Judy's desire to protect me from myself. Oddly, I feel myself blush. I gave Judy the job, yet here I am trying to solve it under her nose.

"Sorry," I say.

My mother glances in my direction. The words don't come easily or likely often enough from my mouth.

"Let me handle things, OK? I'm a good PI and you know it." *Huff, puff.* "Let me do my job. I'm planning to," *huff, puff,* "be up in the area tomorrow. If you want, we can meet for coffee before I head south. Three o'clock at the McDonalds?" *Huff, puff.*

"Sure," I say, "and thanks."

I end the call, put the phone back into the cup holder.

"A sorry and a thank you? My, Tatum Rose, it's nice to see you use your manners for some people." From the corner of my eye, I see my mother studying my face. I grimace.

After dropping Mama off at her house, I breathe a sigh of relief. The woman has the uncanny ability to make me feel guilty just by one of her looks and in short, simple sentences. When I was young and still believed I'd someday grow up to be just like her, this was more anxiety-provoking than today. But still, it never feels good to disappoint the woman that gave birth to you.

I turn on the radio, find a station playing old Irish reels and crank it up. My car practically shudders in embarrassment, but the fast, foot stomping music keeps my mind from going back to the dark days surrounding Max, and I'm grateful for that.

Turning the car toward Highgate, I decide to drop in again, or rather for the first time, at Patty's trailer and see what I can find. Rain starts misting, and the wipers squeal across the windshield in slow motion. Dark clouds have moved in, and the sky suddenly feels much closer, dark and oppressive. Cranking the heater, I consider stopping at the local cup and cone place in the center of Swanton village but force myself past. I haven't been sleeping well as it is. Probably best to lay off the caffeine for a while.

I've just put the turn signal on and am about to make the turn off of Route 78 into the trailer park when I hear the loud blast of a horn behind me. I jump, hands clutching the wheel. Looking in the rearview mirror, I expect to see a big, black pickup with twin smokestacks. Instead, an SUV filled with teens gyrating to music I can't hear zooms past. I bite my lip then drive slowly through the park to Patty's trailer.

My heart has resumed its normal rhythm by the time I approach the door of the mobile home. It's another flimsy aluminum storm door, a twin to the one at the incorrect trailer last night. I open it and am rewarded with a creak and then a squeak. Knocking on the wooden door, I glance around the yard. Lilac bushes, just as the neighbor mentioned, huddle in front of the house. I imagine their sweet smell in May and shiver as the icy mist finds its way down my coat collar. A dog barks somewhere else in the park, and I can smell the piney, smoky fragrance of a newly lit fire in the air.

I knock again. No answer. The house is dark but drapes are undrawn. I glance at the mobile homes to the left and the right. No one peeking out the windows this time. Retracing my steps to the driveway, I duck around the back of the house. Standing on tiptoes, I'm still too short to see in. Sophie wouldn't have a problem, her six-foot legs making everything easier. I alternate feeling bad for myself and checking around the yard for something that might make a good stepstool. The area is fairly bare. A clothesline, which I'd guess hasn't been used in a decade, sags near the far edge of the property. Shrubs line both sides of the yard offering a modicum of

privacy from the neighbors. An assortment of flower
pots are carelessly tumbled in a small pile near what
looks like an outdoor campfire ring. I walk over,
checking both sides of the yard again for neighbors, and
help myself to the largest pot.

Turning it upside down, I plunk it near the window
I was just trying to look through, and am rewarded with
a clear view into the trailer. It's dark though, and my
reflection is all that I can see. Cupping my hands around
my face, I press my nose to the glass. Before me is a
small kitchen, dirty dishes piled high on a small counter.
Combination dining area/pantry takes up the other
corner of the room.

Grabbing the flower pot, I move on to the next
window. This one reveals a nondescript bathroom, small
and untidy. A myriad of beauty products are strewn on
the sink. A blow dryer is propped on the back of the
toilet, a stack of warehouse-sized toilet paper rolls, still
in plastic wrapper, stands near the center of the room and
dirty clothes make up an impressively large pile near the
far wall. Not much of a housekeeper, but thankfully
that's not yet a crime. I think about my own office and
the administrative work—filing, photocopying and
record keeping—that's spread out on the big table
waiting for a certain someone to make time for it.

The low buzzing sound comes louder from the next
room, a bedroom. It's faint but loud enough to hear
without pressing my ear to the window. I can't see
anything in this room, my vision blocked by thick
curtains. Should I try the window? Judy's words about
the possibility of losing my businesses come back to me,
but I give the window a little nudge anyway. What are

the chances it will actually be unlocked?

There's a squeak then a groan and then the window opens surprisingly wide. A horrible smell comes from the room, and I gag and step back reflexively, nearly losing my balance on the flower pot. My fingers dig into the window sill, and the buzzing becomes louder.

Suddenly, I recognize the sound and without control my gut starts contracting, and I lean over and lose the remains of my last meal on the ground near a rhododendron. *Flies.* Thick and droning with thread-like legs and tissue paper wings, they are buzzing around the room.

In an instant the memories flood my brain: Max's apartment; the same smell and sound. Flies, with their tiny tentacle legs and myriad eyes, dirty and scuttling and shimmering in a cloud in the room. I'd pushed open the door, walked inside, calling my brother's name. Known that something was wrong as soon as my feet passed the threshold. I remember the heat in the enclosed space and the way that the walls seemed to contract until it was just me and the smell and sound. That unmistakable scent that had stayed in my nostrils for days afterward.

And then I'd found my kid brother, beautiful, creative Max, curled in a fetal position on the floor near the couch, needle on the floor next to him, eyes rolled back in his head.

And flies, flies, flies everywhere.

CHAPTER TWENTY-TWO

I wipe my mouth on my sleeve now, rise unsteadily to my feet. The flower pot is overturned. I right it, step on it again and, without giving myself time to think better of it, pull my body through the open window. The sound in the room is nearly as loud as a plane in the small space. The sill snags my pant leg, and I jerk at it, pulling the curtains from the rod in my haste. The thin metal bar crashes down, knocking over a lamp into a pile of laundry. I pull my t-shirt up over my nose and follow the sound of the flies.

The room is cold, as cold as the air outside, and a light is on in the closet across the room. An unmade bed takes up most of the room and a bureau with half the drawers open squats near the door. A bare light bulb protrudes from the ceiling of the closet which is positioned beyond an awkwardly placed end table. Nail polish bottles, wrinkled magazines and a can of diet soda take up most of the space on the table. Flies congregate on the soda can and when I draw close to the closet, swarm upward from the floor. The smell, even through my shirt, is overpowering, and I worry for a minute that I'm going to start heaving again. I take another couple deep breaths through my mouth and try not to think past my next motion.

Crouching, I approach the closet door and pull it back. At first, it's difficult to see anything. The bare bulb is so far away from the floor that most of it is shadowed. Mismatched hangers line a single cheap plastic bar above, most of them missing clothes. Sneakers, a pair of scuffed boots with pointed heels and a few pair of cheap flip flops are scattered around on the faded green carpet.

And there, in the middle of yet another pile of dirty clothes, is the victim. A cat, plump and fluffy with its mouth dropped open. Flies cover every orifice, buzzing busily in and out of the mouth, mostly hollow eye sockets, and leathery looking ears. I gag again and pull back from the small space.

Stumbling backward, I launch myself out of the window, the sill scraping skin off my belly on the way down. The air outside smells incredible, and I suck in great gasps of it, fresh and clean and alive. I sit on the flower pot for a few minutes, trying to get my bearings, attempting and failing to push away thoughts of Max and the apartment and the flies.

It takes fifteen long minutes before I'm ready to go back in. During that time part of my brain first whispers and then screams at me to get out of here, to contact the police and let them take over. The voice also reminds me, repeatedly, that I could lose my security business for this. Trespassing. Breaking and entering. Tampering with a potential crime scene. Because while the dead cat isn't necessarily a crime that would be prosecuted (maybe Kitty died from old age?), I don't know what else awaits me in Patty's trailer.

Despite the pleas of this rational portion of my brain, I am pulling myself back over the sill and into the dark bedroom. This time I lift my body upward and avoid re-scraping my stomach, which is still stinging.

I cross through the room quickly now, opening and closing the hollow core door leading into a narrow hallway. Three doors, two are closed. The one on the left must be the bathroom that I saw. I open the door and see that I'm right. No odd smells or sounds coming from here. I do a quick search anyway, pulling back the shower curtain and then replacing it, opening a miniature linen closet, which is surprisingly tidy, and closing the door again. I step back into the hallway. The next door, on the right, is partially open, and I push it the rest of the way. The curtains here are open, and dull light from outdoors outlines an older model computer perched on a pressboard desk, two leaning banker's boxes stacked one on the other in the corner. A closet holds some coats and smells of mothballs.

Retreating into the hallway, I open the final door. Another closet, this one stuffed with garbage bags full of what appear to be more clothes. Patty is obviously interested in her appearance, and from what I've seen her tastes veer toward the 80s. Or maybe these are on their way to a thrift shop somewhere?

The hallway opens into the living room/dining room area and the small kitchen that I first saw from outdoors. The rest of the house is unremarkable. Outdated furnishings, old blue shag carpet that's seen better days, and a few interestingly placed bits of generic artwork. I open drawers in the kitchen, but they reveal only normal kitchen-y things: spatulas, cutlery, a few books of matches, and empty ashtrays. The fridge reveals a lot of diet soda, a few crusty condiment bottles and a loaf of saggy white bread.

No family photos dot the walls in any of the rooms, which is odd. I retrace my steps to the office and turn on the computer. That little voice pipes up in my head again, but whatever. In for a pinch, in for a pound, right? The computer takes several long minutes to awake from its technological stupor, and I spend the time pilfering the banker's boxes. Old tax forms, letters from an attorney involved in a worker's comp case and other boring personal paperwork are shoved in at random. Though on second thought, the tax paperwork could be enlightening. I remove the rubber band holding the packet together and peruse the file. Patty J. Commo worked at Stevens' Auto Shop as a secretary.

From the job title alone, I can tell what type of place this is: good ole boys with pinup calendars and locker room jokes galore. Political correctness dictates that the term "secretary" is an outdated term. "Office Manager," or "Administrative Assistant," or even "Clerk" is much more PC.

The computer monitor has finally come alive, the desktop screen filled with icons of games. Lots and lots of games. And probably every single shortcut to every single bit of software installed since it first came out of its factory-delivered box.

I start meandering through files. Unlike her home, the digital folders are neat and tidy, even listed in alphabetical order and in chronological order by month and year.

Nice, Patty.

I scroll through, not even sure what I'm looking for. I see older tax records, personal letters to a sister who, upon further inspection, is in a prison in Arkansas, and a lot of kitty pictures. The cat in the photos is glossy and well-kept, its belly rounded and its eyes bright and a bit snobbish, in that feline way. Definitely the same cat that the flies are munching. If this woman loved her cat so much, why is it lying dead in her closet?

A jiggle of the front door handle sends me darting out of the room and into the hallway. The shadow of a man stands at the door, and then the shadow knocks, and I almost jump in the air. The sound is loud and ricochets around the small rooms. I run back into the office, pull the plug on the computer and huddle behind it. A flash drive pokes my side, and I pull it free of the rear USB port and tuck it in my pocket. Then I half crawl toward the office door and into the hallway to see if the figure is still there.

It's gone.

Crap. Crap. Crap!

Crab walking down the hall, I stay low in case the guy has the same brilliant idea I did to peek in all the exterior windows. I think of the flower pot, the wind blowing through the rear bedroom.

Stupid, Tayt. Really dumb.

Now what am I going to do?

My finger goes to my mouth, and I automatically start gnawing a hangnail then think of where my hands have been in the past hour and drop it immediately.

"Anyone home?" a low voice says from outside. Which room? Bathroom, I think. I can't make out the rest of the sentence because the voice is moving toward the rear of the trailer. It seems to stop mid-sentence, and I picture the man surveying the flower pot and then the open window, curtains blowing in the breeze. The smell alone must be making him curious. I shiver, thinking about the flies, then duck and run toward the front door. If I can get it open without much noise, and he's still distracted by the smell and window from around back, I can make it to my car and get out of here before he even starts to look for me.

I ease the lock open and hold my breath as the door handle pulls forward in my palm. Except, it doesn't. I pull harder, but there's no movement. Finally I grip the sucker with both hands and jerk. I'm rewarded with a loud squawk.

I don't wait to find out if Shadow Man heard it too. Hustling, I yank the door closed behind me, wasting another few precious seconds, and sprint toward the car. Fumbling with keys in my pocket, I don't see the vehicle of the man. I'm nearly to the car. Feet pounding on a bed of dry leaves, I rattle through the keys on the ring, trying to find the right one. There!

And then a hand clamps down on my shoulder.

CHAPTER TWENTY-THREE

I whirl around, hands up in a protective stance. My keys go flying in the grass, and my ponytail nearly blinds me, the tip slashing across my face.

"Whoa," the voice says. It's one that I recognize.

"Ez?" Then, "What are you doing here?"

He grins at me, hands still up in a show of peace-I-want-no-trouble.

"Um, I'm not sure, but I think I am the one who should be asking you that. Did you just sprint from this person's house after breaking in through a back window?" He puts his hands down. The grin stays firmly in place.

I take a couple of deep breaths, make a big deal out of searching for my keys to hide my red cheeks.

"I didn't break in," I say, finally facing him again, keys mashed into a fist. "The window was unlocked. And I thought the lady was dead. I was just trying to help."

"Oh, uh-huh. So it's OK to break into dead people's houses?" Pause. He goes on without waiting for a response. "She's not, is she? Dead?"

I sigh. "No, she's not. Just her cat."

He frowns, eyes darkening. I like animals, some

more than others. Ezra, though, is a big-time animal lover and has been since we were kids. He was always bringing some mangy mutt or bedraggled cat to our house. Mama couldn't say no to Ezra. And Jack traveled so much that the cat or dog or bird, or whatever it was, had found a new home with some family in the neighborhood by the time he returned. Mama could talk a traveling salesman into buying his own merchandise, so this didn't take a lot of effort on her part. And for Ezra, it was just one more reason to love living with us. His own mother would have drowned the animals while he slept and told him they died of natural causes.

"What happened to the cat?" Ezra asks.

I'm tempted to sugar coat it, like I used to with Max. Once, when we were playing with a fat little brown toad, Max accidently dropped it, the tiny body impaled on an unfortunately positioned stick. I scooped it up and ran to the big field nearby, pretending to do CPR and then tossing its lifeless body into the grass as my kid brother trudged up behind me bawling his eyes out.

"See? Did you see him, Max? He's perfectly fine. I fixed him up good as new, and he just went hopping off in that tall grass to find his mom and dad."

My brother was young and naïve, and when he turned his tear-streaked face to me, it was shining with hope.

"Really? Promise, Tatum?"

I hugged his thin shoulders. "Sure," I said, hoping he wouldn't see my fingers crossed behind my back.

But Ezra is not my little brother, and he's not three years old. I swallow, hard.

"I'm not sure," I say. "I didn't see any wounds on

it." Then, "And what are you even doing here?"

Ezra is looking toward the back of the trailer. He glances back to me, rubs his chin. I can't get used to this new facial hair thing. It looks so un-Ezra.

"I was calling on Mrs. Wilson who lives down there." He points to a neighboring trailer. "I saw your jalopy, I mean, uh, car, and thought I'd stop and say hello."

"Calling on her? What is this, the 18th Century?"

"It's a term that the brothers use. It's a little old-fashioned," he shrugs, "but you know me. I like old-fashioned stuff." He scratches at his jaw. "Mrs. Wilson is newly widowed. I met with her briefly on Sunday. She pulled me aside after mass, told me she was having some problems and asked if I would stop in sometime this week to visit her."

"And priests, I mean, brothers, still do that kind of thing?"

"Sure, when we have enough man power at the home church. It's nice to see people in their own environments, and it makes them more comfortable. Though we usually travel in twos when there are single women involved—even new widows who are about the age of our great-grandmothers." Ezra looks at her trailer again. "Brother Charlie was sick this morning, though, so I was going to pinch hit on my own. She must have forgotten our appointment; I rang the bell three times and no answer. Her car's gone too."

"What'd she want to talk to you about?"

He looks at me, a slow smile starting at one corner of his mouth.

"You're too nosy. You know that, right? Anyway,

you'd probably be more interested in what I know about this lady." He nods toward Patty's trailer. "I might know her from mass, or I might not. I can't share that type of information with just anyone and everyone, you know." His smile widens, and I whack his shoulder.

"Please. I'm hardly 'anyone' or 'everyone.' Besides, I'm here on legal business." I stand a little straighter. "She has a grandmother that's worried about her."

Ezra's slow smile turns to a full-on grin. He jerks his head toward the back of the trailer.

"Nice try, Tatum. The old "Granny's worried," tactic, huh? You forget that I'm a man of the cloth. I can smell lies a mile away. And you, sweetheart, are far from smelling rose-like." For the second time in days, my stomach does a little jig. I'm not sure if this is due to being caught mid-lie—a talent I consider myself quite advanced in—or the word *sweetheart*.

Ezra pats my arm. "Don't worry, though. I'll let you make it up to me by buying me lunch.

My eyebrows shoot up.

"Buying you what?"

He nods.

"Go back and put away your step stool, Nancy Drew. I'll call this in to the state police. It's going to look a lot less suspicious coming from me, and anyway, I won't be lying," Ezra says as though I was about to accuse him of that. Or maybe it's just his guilty Catholic conscience. "I'll just duck in and take a quick look. I would have eventually gotten the window open myself. Probably. Most likely." He heads toward the open window, sliding in easily with his long limbs. For a heavyset guy, Ezra is surprisingly nimble.

I don't wait for a second invitation. After returning the pot to its original position, I double check the area where I got sick. Most of the remains have leeched away into the sandy soil, but I scuff some more dirt and dry leaves over the spot, just in case. I return to the front step, and Ezra joins me moments later, his breathing slightly increased.

"That place is a dump. And the cat looks like it's been dead at least a day or two, don't you think?" I'm no expert with dead bodies, but it doesn't seem that it's deteriorated past the point of no return. Which I'd guess would be three days.

Ezra's face is hard, lines showing where there are usually smiling dimples. I knew that the dead cat would bother him. I nod in response but don't say anything. Better to not incriminate myself further at this point.

"Did you see how it died?"

"Poison? I don't know. I didn't see any blood," Ezra shakes his head. "You'd better get going before the trooper gets here. We can finish our conversation at the restaurant. Which brings up a question: Where are you taking me?"

A half hour later, we're seated in a booth at a local pizza joint. The waitress has just slid a steaming pie into the center of the table, and my mouth waters in response, a fact that amazes me. After that noxious odor, I'm surprised I can even think of food. But the double workouts from yesterday must have bumped up my caloric output. I wasn't even hungry until I walked in; the warm cheesy-tomato scent that pervades every pizza parlor on earth washes over me.

We each grab a piece and chew simultaneously, the unspoken waiting until our bellies are full. Finally, over sips of soda and half-hearted nibbles at third slices, I update Ezra about my father's case, Alinah and my suspicions about the house across from my office and Doug, the suspected pimp and human trafficker. I also add in this new job with Patty which may not be worth my time at this point. It will be only another dozen hours or so before the police can start an official investigation, and after finding the dead cat, maybe even that window has grown smaller.

Ezra, who has been silent through all of this, finally speaks.

"I have a friend who works with immigration in the Burlington office. He might be able to help you out with Alinah." He sips from his nearly-empty soda, catches the eye of a waitress with a crinkly smile, and a refill appears within seconds.

He pulls a pen and comment card from a little plastic holder on the table and scribbles a name and number on it then slides the paper across to me.

"Give him a call. Seth's a good guy—if there's a way to help you out, he'll do it."

"Thanks," I say. "There's a chance that Alinah might be open to running. At least I hope so. She won't involve the police at this point, and while I'd love to tip them off, I don't want to do anything to make things worse for her." I sip my soda. "If that happens, she'll need help getting out of the country, and fast. I don't want her to go to prison, and I can offer her a place to stay temporarily, if she calls me. What can Seth do, exactly? Could he speed up the paperwork needed to get her back home?

"I'd hope so." Ezra sits back in the padded booth which squeaks under his weight. "It didn't go so well for the women that were found in the trafficking ring in Williston though, did it?"

I'm not sure why the fact that he's heard of this is startling. I guess I think of him as being completely cut off in a monastery.

"No, not at all." I think about the articles I read.

"How's your father doing?" Ezra switches topics, and my back stiffens automatically. I try to pretend that I'm just getting ready to stretch.

"Fine, I guess."

"Really?" Ezra pauses, sips his fresh soda. "And your mom?"

I wave my hand side to side. "Not so great. I don't know why the woman even cares at this point, I honestly don't. You'd think after all of these years and after all he put her through ..."

Ezra is shaking his head, a slow side to side, like a mournful dog.

"You don't get it, do you, Tayt?"

"Get what?"

"She's still in love with him. Isn't it obvious? You can see it in her face, hear it in her voice when she talks about him. It's kind of sweet, really."

I snort.

"Sweet? Being a doormat for some creep who screws up your life and then leaves you to pick up the pieces is something, but sweet isn't it." I slap a hand down on the table, the red pepper jar bouncing. Ezra's eyebrows rise and the smile has faded slightly. His tanned, calloused fingers flick mine gently.

"Well, it depends how you look at it, I guess. There is this little thing called forgiveness, you know. Maybe your mother has decided to be the better person, let go of the anger and enjoy the rest of her years with peace. Or maybe she can see in her older wisdom that your father wasn't the only one to blame for the demise of their marriage." He holds up a hand as I start to blurt hot words from my lips without thinking.

"I'm not saying that what he did was right. Leaving wasn't right. Moving in with Chelsea wasn't right. But have you ever considered that you might be putting a little too much of the blame on him? Your mother was dealing with her own demons. I'm not saying that she drove him to it, that she caused him to leave your family. Just that he's not all bad. Not evil. It takes two to tango, and her drinking didn't leave him with much room for ..."

I stand up. Childishly, I want to clap my hands over my ears, *Lalallaaalaaaaaaa, I'm not listening!* Instead, I throw a twenty on the table.

"I'm not really in the mood to discuss my family dynamics today, Ez," I draw out the word "my" to make him feel as excluded as possible. "If you want to psychoanalyze someone, maybe you should start with your own parents. There's something to write your first book about: *How my Psychotic Upbringing Drove me to the Church.*" The words taste hot and rancid in my throat, but I can't stop them.

"You might have lived in my house, but Jack is not your father and Lillian isn't your mom. So please, save me the pathetic insight into my parents' relationship."

I look at his face, expecting red anger. Instead, his eyes are soft, his face relaxed. His breathing is even, normal. *In, out. In, out.* For some reason, even this infuriates me. I sling my scarf around my throat, make the knot too tight and nearly gag. Ezra grabs my hand before I move down the aisle between the cherry red booths.

"I'm sorry, Tayt. I shouldn't have brought it up. It's none of my business." His eyes are searching every inch of my face. "You're right. I've got enough skeletons of my own to deal with without diving into your closet."

His hand is warm, and two Band-Aids crisscross his palm, likely from blisters created from hours of painting and carpentry at the Shrine. He tugs gently, and something horrible happens. Before I can stop myself, hot, salty tracks cascade down my face. I'm crying for the second time in two days. This is truly a record. I don't think I've cried this much since Max ...

"Forgive me?"

Ezra asks, pulling me down into the booth beside him. It sinks in the middle, rolling us closer together. His arm is heavy around my shoulders, and I turn and bury my wet, slobbery face into his neck. Instantly his t-shirt is soaked, my gasps and mewls simultaneously humiliating and liberating. Something tight and strangling in my chest claws its way free. I can literally feel heaviness lifting.

"I'm so sorry," I say, voice muffled and stilted by sobs. "I didn't mean any of what I said. Well, maybe about my father, but not you. You're part of our family, Ezra. I didn't mean what I said about your parents."

He rubs my back a little, puts his face down near mine and whispers in my ear, "Well, they are pretty psychotic."

I laugh a little, then push away, grabbing blindly for the chrome napkin dispenser. Mopping my face, I run a hand through my hair, untangling it before finally looking at my best friend.

"Why do you put up with me?" This isn't the first time I've asked the question, and it's not the first he's given me the same answer.

"You're stuck with me, Tayt. Like it or not, I'm the proverbial neglected dog that followed you home. You gave me some food, rubbed my belly and now look: stuck for life. You should be more careful who you show mercy to."

I roll my eyes. "Mercy is hardly in my repertoire."

"It is actually. You just don't see it."

"All set here, Father?" The waitress stands near the booth, and I'm suddenly conscious of how wrong this must look to her. I wiggle out, cheeks red.

"He's not a priest yet," I say, then feel even stupider.

"We're old friends, Kate," says Ezra.

"Mmmhmmmm," she says, glancing from him to me and back. "I can see that, darling."

Now it's Ezra's turn to blush, but of course he doesn't, just grins at her and gives a wink. "See you at Mass on Sunday?"

"Oh, I'll be there. Gramma wouldn't miss it. She might miss most of what Father Benoir is saying in the liturgy, but she won't miss the service."

"Ask her to keep the snores down this week, huh?"

Kate laughs. I smile. Ezra grins. One big, happy, pizza-lovin' family.

CHAPTER TWENTY-FOUR

There's a shady-looking internet café on the corner of Pearl Street and Main in downtown Burlington. I find myself in the city every few weeks running errands and getting some good Indian food.

A parking spot three blocks away from the café opens up, and I nab it, feed the meter and walk to the shop, which is just starting to sprout customers. College kids from the nearby University of Vermont campus (Groovy U'vy) roll in, hair mussed, faces sleepy, backpacks and messenger bags stuffed. They group together in one part of the café, as though programmed to stay together as a unit, even off campus. Between yawns, they talk and joke. The rest of us working stiffs and out of work jerks stick to the other side of the room. I glance around as I wait for my computer to wake from sleep mode. Chipped linoleum, popcorn ceiling sporting spitballs, bits of gum and the smell of old coffee make this a sad shadow of the Starbucks just down the road. Still, Starbucks doesn't have computers to use, computers that, unlike my laptop, won't be at risk for searching if this case goes south.

I insert the flash drive I got from Patty's computer and wait again for the driver to upload. Sipping from my paper cup, I make a face. Definitely not Starbucks. I'm not a coffee snob by any means; I just like my coffee to slide easily down my throat.

A light flashes, and a window pops up announcing that the files on the flash drive are ready to be explored.

I open the first folder and gape. Thirty file folder icons line the screen in tidy rows. Each is broken down by date, prefaced by the letters SAS.

Two mouse clicks and the first folder opens to reveal a lot of boring-looking documents. SAS, it turns out, is for Stevens' Auto Shop. These, I realize as I scroll through the list, must be the backup work for Patty's day job.

Clicking back to the main screen, I go through the folders again. Every one is similar; Patty is meticulous, if not in her housekeeping habits, then definitely in her work. It takes me a few long minutes to figure out her filing system, even so, but there's nothing incriminating here. The bills came in, were paid and went back out. There's definitely profit. Miller apparently runs a successful business but nothing that looks suspicious to me.

I'm about to close the window when I see a single document on the flash drive all by its lonesome. I look at the title, but it is a string of letters and numbers that don't make sense.

I double click the icon, and a one-page Word document opens. The first line is a string of dates, the second column various numbers, many in the tens of thousands. Money, I'm guessing. There is a third line but little filled in. A couple of fragment sentences, "delivery to Montreal?" and "Materials?," but that's it.

I roll my shoulders, sit back in the molded plastic chair. Useless. And now I somehow have to get this back into her trailer, in the off-chance she plans to return. Even if she doesn't, Miller or someone who works there knows that she keeps the backup records at her place and is bound to come looking for them. Maybe that's why her place was such a wreck. Maybe someone trashed it and killed her cat in the process, as a warning. Goose bumps pop out along my arms and neck. Most businesses—even legitimate ones—don't want this kind of information just floating around out in the world.

I sit up again as another little yellow folder catches my eye. "Personal," it reads. Opening it, I see another string of folders. This woman is beyond digitally organized and bordering on obsessive.

Folders named "Mr. Fluffy" (her cat?), "Vacation 2011," and "Photos" march up and down the screen interspersed with other normal sounding files. Still, the nosy in me is curious. I click on the photos file and wait a few seconds while the computer changes the standard photo icons into little thumbnail images.

Patty takes a lot of selfies. There's one in front of a tree, another of her thumb out "Way to go, Dude!" in front of a restaurant on the beach offering fried clams, more of her posed in various awkward angles as she tries to capture a flattering shot with the camera at the end of her arm.

Not an easy task.

I scroll through the rest of the pictures but find nothing interesting. There are some non-selfie shots: Patty sitting at some bar, posing with a couple of scary-looking biker guys, Patty's newly painted toenails (complete with tiny flowers!), Patty's depressing-looking rainy vacation to Atlantic City. One semi-hot guy—hot in a slightly grungy, leftover head banger sort of way—appears in multiple photos for a period of time. He and Patty smile, sunburned at a little plastic table in Atlantic City, and there are a few others where he's kissing her cheek or she's smooching his bicep. But then those are gone. The tragic end of a love story gone wrong? Or was their relationship more of a wham-bam-thank-you-ma'am type?

The selfies, though, those got my attention. There's one reason that people take these photos: social networking. I follow the directions at the computer station to get online and Google Patty Commo and Facebook. Of course, there are a crap-load of listings. But when I narrow down the search by adding Vermont, only a few show up. One Patty is in her fifties and has a head of short grayish hair. Another is too young but, just like Goldielocks, the third one is just right.

I have never understood the draw to Facebook and other social networking sites. To me, it seems like a lot of work for very little reward. "Look at me! Look what I'm doing!" as though everyone posting is stuck forever at age nine and needs an audience to eat their lunch or go on vacation.

Patty, though, is a Facebook champ. Seriously, if there was a contest for most hours logged, she might win. Apparently a fan of online games, she prefers those featuring kitties and another game with colorful bubbles in it. I check the dates of her last game: this morning at seventeen past nine.

Bingo.

While I'm on her page (has the woman ever heard of privacy settings?), I also scroll through her friends list, making a note of those people who have commented most often and most frequently. These are friends to follow up with in real life. I also look for any current images or maybe even a slip from Patty as to where she might be hiding out, but there's nothing. Apparently she isn't that stupid. Just to use up the rest of the minutes I paid for, I click on a few of her friends' pictures.

"Your time's up," a scruffy-looking twenty year-old says, tapping me on the shoulder. I shake off his touch automatically, and he holds both palms up, looking defensive.

"Hey, hey. I'm just letting you know, man. Don't shoot the messenger."

I grunt in response. Just as I'm about to exit, I find one more friend who recently logged in. Jill Moyers who, conveniently, works here in Burlington. Jotting that info down, I log off.

Gathering my scrap paper, the flash drive and keys, I meander through the busy aisles to the register to make sure I'm all paid up. Just enough time to pop in at Jill's office before it closes, provided the insurance company keeps regular hours.

CHAPTER TWENTY-FIVE

A minute later I emerge into a day that is October-beautiful: pure blue sky stretched with gauze clouds around the edges, autumn sunshine filtering through rusted tree leaves. There's a smile on my lips and a little fissure of excitement in my chest.

Climbing into the car, I retrieve an older model GPS from underneath the passenger seat and plug it into the cigarette lighter. It blinks to life, orange screen reminding me that I shouldn't use this technology while operating a moving vehicle. I skip the rest of the welcome screen junk while using my phone to locate the street address of Patty's friend Jill, who works at Hymer Insurance Company, just minutes away. Plugging the address into the GPS, I put on my seatbelt (thanks for the reminder, GPS, I never would have been smart enough to do that on my own!) and turn east toward South Burlington.

Traffic is heavy this time of day, people getting out of work and heading home, college students—those lucky enough to have cars—cruising toward one of the surrounding towns to catch a movie or grab dinner outside the center of the city. Following the stop and go traffic, I listen to the GPS voice drone on about merging traffic. When I make a wrong turn, I imagine, not for the first time, the tinny voice telling me, "Not that way, you stupid idiot. Do I have to take the wheel and show you?" Instead she says, "Now, make a U-turn," which I do.

The rest of the ride is uneventful, and I arrive shortly in the parking area of the insurance company. Not an overly successful place judging from the outside. The lot is overgrown with weeds and brush around the edges, as though the woody parts are trying to reclaim the area. The pavement is cracked and broken in several places, and the building itself, squat and brown, looks neglected.

I head for the glass door. There are still lights on inside.

Jill Moyers herself answers the door. I know this, not because I ask, but because she wears a small gold pin over her left breast which states her name, followed by, "Insurance Claims Officer." She holds her hand out, all toothy grin until I tell her why I'm there. The hand falls limply to her side, and she points to a small kitchenette off of the waiting room.

"Wait in there. I'll be with you in a minute."

I nod and smile, pretending not to be offended when I'm not offered a beverage or foot rub despite the little placard hanging in the waiting room that boasts, "Hymer Insurance: Where You'll be Treated like Royalty!" I'm not feeling particularly royal.

Jill reappears moments later. She's about Patty's age, mid-forties, and looks like she's lived a hard life. Spider web lines around her eyes and brown spots dotting her chest tell me she enjoys the sun protection-free.

"What do you want?" she says bluntly, cutting out the pleasantries.

"I hope you save all your nice manners for potential customers," I say, but she doesn't smile.

"I'm looking for your friend, Patty Commo. I ..." *found you on Facebook* doesn't sound very professional. "My research led me to you."

A cocked eyebrow is the only response.

"Can you tell me when you saw Patty last? Or where she is now?"

"Yeah, right. I'm going to rat out my best friend to some private investigator."

I start to remind her that I'm not a PI, but she waves away the rest of my sentence like it's an annoying fly.

"Whatever. Patty doesn't need this right now. She's in a bad place, and you just want to ...What is it you plan to do?"

I go with a hunch.

"I know that Patty's in trouble. Her grandmother is really worried about her. And I know about Miller Stevens. Whatever you can tell me ..."

Her abnormally tanned face pales slightly at the mention of Stevens.

"You know about him?"

I nod, hoping she won't ask how.

She calls him a name that would turn my granny's skin maroon, spitting the word out like it's an errant bug. "He's put Patty in a real bad spot. Real bad."

Careful, Tayt. One slip and Jill will know how little I actually know about what's going on.

"He's a suspect in another case I'm working on." *Nonchalant. Bordering on disinterested.*

Jill's eyes fairly glitter in response. She must really hate the guy.

"Really? Hmmm," she pauses, rubbing an acrylic-nailed finger under her bottom lip, her eyes looking behind us into the main office. "I'd love to see Miller get nailed."

I smile. "I can make that happen," I say, then worry that it sounds too smarmy. Jill doesn't seem to notice. She stares vacantly, and I can almost see the tiny wheels and mechanisms working behind her forehead. Finally, she nods.

"Patty worked for Miller at her last job."

"The garage?" I blurt out, then kick myself. *Let her tell the story.*

Jill lets out an exaggerated sigh. "Yeah. Patty was the receptionist/gopher/peon there for a couple of years. She had a little crush on him, no big deal. I mean, who of us hasn't wanted to get skanky with the boss and move on up the ladder, right?" She snorts a laugh, and I force a chuckle. *Of course! That's exactly how promotions work.*

"Anyway, turns out he wasn't interested in her, but he didn't mind screwing her for a couple months for fun. Patty isn't stupid, she knew what was going on, just chose to overlook it. For a while.

"But then Miller gets drunk one night, I mean tanked." She draws the word out as though it has three syllables. "Tells Patty about his real money maker. The garage is good money, don't get me wrong …but Miller has higher goals I guess. Have you seen his spread down at the lake? It must have cost close to a mil."

I nod.

"Anyway," Jill's voice lowers to a whisper even though we are the only ones in the room, "it turns out Miller is involved in some sort of smuggling ring. At first Patty thought it was drugs—you know, he likes his pot—but who of us doesn't?" Another benevolent smile and nod from me. I may have missed my calling in life as a therapist.

"But it wasn't dope. Wasn't drugs at all. It was ..." her voice breaks off and she glances behind us, out into the empty main office, and then leans closer to me. Her breath smells like pink bubblegum and old peanut butter. "Women. You know, foreigners? For prostitution. He ships them in from God knows where and sets them up in houses with pimps and everything. Can you believe it?

"When Patty told me this my mouth just about fell to the floor. I mean, who even knew that that still happened? Mail order brides like from the 1800s. Crazy. Meanwhile perfectly good looking women like Patty and I are like clawing, I mean literally clawing sometimes, to find good men on girls' night out. And here are men paying for sex—it just makes no sense to me."

I'm not sure which is more ironic: that Jill is offended that men would prefer to pay for sex with someone other than herself and Patty or that she considers these "good men." Still, a small glow of yellow satisfaction pools in my belly.

Finally, finally, I have a solid link between Miller Stevens and a sex trafficking ring. And if Sam comes through and can prove that this is somehow tied in with Jack, I might soon be able to get Miller put away for a really long time.

A smile widens on my cheeks. This time, it's not forced.

CHAPTER TWENTY-SIX

Interstate 89 is a pretty drive for a highway. It curls through picturesque glens showcasing ruby-red barns and around towns surrounding a single white steeple like all the postcards show. A law against billboards ensures plenty of country to see at every turn.

The section of the interstate I'm driving now, however, is somewhat dull, and I catch my eyes closing halfway more than once.

I signal and pull over at the next rest area. I do some shoulder rolls on my way into the small building, reading signs instructing that dogs be cleaned up after, that no smoking is allowed in the building and that all valuables should be locked in vehicles.

The room is crammed with maps and display cases of Vermont products like maple syrup, photos of cows munching happily on grass, and advertisements for Ben & Jerry's, the un-official state ice cream, all crowded together. Signs direct visitors to vending machines and restrooms, which I gladly follow.

When I return to the entry area, a man is standing beside the high desk looking down at some paperwork. He glances up, nods and points me in the direction of complimentary carafes of Green Mountain Coffee, another state treasure. I thank him and stir in creamer and sugar while he talks about the weather, the start of hunting season and asks where I'm from.

When I tell him, he nods. "Murder up there in the news, huh?" He waits for a nod. "Terrible thing. Always wonder what our world is coming to—what our *state* is coming to—when you see something like that happen."

I clear my throat, retrieve a bent photo of Patty from my back pocket and lay it on the counter. "I'm Tayt Waters, and I run a securities firm. This is a long shot I know, but I'm looking for this woman, Patty Commo. Any chance you've seen her?"

The man, "Gary" it says on a blue bar pin over his left pocket, studies the picture. He taps a finger on it, then shakes his head slowly.

"Don't think so. Sorry."

"No problem," I say. Disappointment squeezes my chest, but I remind myself that it was a longshot.

"Thanks for the coffee," I tell Gary and deposit a dollar into an acrylic donation box. I give a little salute with the cup and get back into the car.

I've just put the car in reverse when Gary jogs out of the rest area building, his steps slow and lumbering. I wait for him to approach the car, cranking my window down.

"That woman you're looking for, I think I did see her. Must've been day before yesterday. Most mornings, when it's slow, I have my break over there," he points to a cluster of picnic tables to the left of the parking area, "read the paper and have my second cup of the day. Thought it was a little strange that she didn't come in, that's why I remember her I guess. Most people need to

191

use the restroom or need a cup to wake them up, you know? But she was just sitting there."

I nod. "What type of car?"

"She was on a bus, a Greyhound. Pretty lightly loaded, most of them are fuller, you know?" Gary continues.

My heartbeat picks up speed.

"Can you remember anything else about her? If she might have been traveling with someone?" I ask.

Gary shakes his head. "No, sorry. I got distracted by the garbage barrel over there." He points behind us to a large metal grated container. "Noticed it was too full and went into the shed to grab more bags. When I came back out the bus was gone. I didn't think much of it at the time, of course."

I nod.

"Thanks so much. If you remember anything else or happen to see her again, would you please give me a call?" I pass one of my business cards out the window to him. He studies it a moment then tucks it into his breast pocket.

"Will do."

The next several miles are used putting together pieces in my mental jigsaw puzzle. My brain is moving much more quickly, thanks to the caffeine rush, spitting information and facts out to me like a well-run popcorn machine at the cinema.

Patty and Miller are connected. Miller and Sam are connected. Miller and Doug are connected to Alinah and Sarjana, and Sarjana is connected to my father in some way.

There are still more questions than answers, though. For one, why would Simon drug my father? Was he hired to do so, and if so, by whom? And why incriminate Jack in any of this?

I dig in my memory bank for anything Miller has ever said to me that would shed light on the dimly lit subject. Nothing comes to mind. No hatred between the two, unfortunately, which would help a lot at this point. Some business deal gone wrong? Maybe a wonky car repair done by Miller's shop that ended up in catastrophe and that Jack threatened Miller with. But my father would have said something to me, to his attorney. And even though, financially, the two men are likely within the same income bracket, socially they're miles apart. It's hard to believe that Jack would have any associations with Miller Stevens, professional or otherwise. Still Sam's words keep niggling at me.

I pass a sign promising that moose are in the area for the next two miles and that drivers should use caution. I slow down slightly and check for a cell phone signal, ignoring the bright orange signs telling me that this is illegal. I call Seth at Immigration again and leave another message.

Do government people ever answer their phones? Are there even real people who work there? I'm starting to wonder. I hope Seth's not on vacation, though the long-winded voicemail woman would tell me if he was, I'm sure. She'd probably notify me of his exact itinerary while away and how he prefers his eggs at breakfast.

Pulling off the exit for Bellows Falls, I head to the Greyhound station. The building is low brick trimmed with green paint. An older woman with frizzy hair is working at the high counter, typing into a computer when I walk through the door.

"Can I help you?" she asks without looking up. Customer service obviously isn't her forte. I remain silent until finally, she glances my way, looking annoyed.

"I hope so. I'm looking for a friend, Patty Commo, who came in on a bus from St. Albans the other day. It would have been Monday night late, or maybe Tuesday sometime."

"Mmmm hmmmm," she is frowning, twin eyebrows pulled together over a pair of brilliant green eyes. Colored contacts? Either that or she is half lizard.

"I'm trying to find her because her grandmother asked me to," I say, putting a worried look on my own face.

"Oh, her grandmother asked you to. Well, isn't that sweet of you." She blows air out of her cheeks, which make little round pillows when filled with breath. "Look, Honey, it's my first day back after vacation. You could talk to Rob or Clark; they worked earlier this week." She points in the direction of two younger guys who've just emerged from the employee-only area.

One of them glances our way and smiles. He's in his mid-twenties, cute and slightly disheveled. I smile back, thank the woman behind the counter and mosey on over.

Rob is friendly and flirty and yes, he remembers Patty once I show him her picture. She'd asked him about a cheap place to stay, he said, and he'd recommended a motel on the outskirts of town. She'd taken a cab.

Rob offers to buy me a drink when he gets off work, but I decline with a smile. Hopefully I won't be here that late.

I pull into the lot of the motel minutes later. The place is a typical low-budget accommodation: slate blue with gray shutters, the paint faded and chipped when illuminated in the car's light beams. Twenty units running along the front of the building, each featuring a pair of cheap white chairs out front and empty pots which in the summer must bloom with some hardy flower. The area is neglected and ugly, from the potholed gravel driveway to the nearby and equally rundown cottage with a neon sign flashing "office."

A scruffy-looking young guy behind the counter barely glances up when the little bell jingles. He stares intently at his computer as though he's just putting the final touches on a formula to cure cancer.

"Hello" I say. "I'm looking for a friend who checked in recently." I decide not to use Patty's name in case she's taken on an alias. Instead, I slide the now slightly crumpled photo across the counter to him. "Can you tell me what room she's in?"

He shakes his head without looking.

I grit my teeth. "Would you mind taking a peek before you say no?"

Twenty-Something sighs heavily, as though I've asked him for a ride to Chicago in his rickshaw. He looks at the photo for about two seconds, then looks away, then back. The dark eyes get wider.

"We don't give out that kind of information about

guests."

I grab a ten dollar bill from my back pocket and slide it over the counter.

"Maybe this will help." The guy just stares. "Look, I'm not asking for a room key, buddy, just a room number. She can decide if she wants to let me in or not."

He glances at the money, rubs a hand over his chin.

"Nope, sorry." He starts to look back to his computer, and I fumble in my pocket again, slipping a second ten onto the chipped surface.

"You sure?"

He looks at the money, then me, then back to the money.

He smiles. His teeth are crooked and stained a little around the edges.

"Yeah, I think I do remember now. Seeing your friend."

"And?"

"And what?" He rubs the side of his nose, pockets the cash. "That's all that twenty bucks gets you. She was in the office. You need more information than that, and it will cost you another—"

I grab his shirt collar and bring his head to the counter so fast that his glasses nearly stay behind.

"Hey, are you freaking crazy?" He whines, and the sound of it makes me want to bash his head again just for the fun of it.

"Do you have a room number or not?"

"Yeah, man. I mean, yes, yes, ma'am," he says, as I pull the fabric tighter.

"I'm losing patience," I say, the fabric of the guy's shirt cutting into his neck enough to make a deep red line. "And your manners could really use some work. Now," I hiss, drawing my face close enough to his to see an ingrown hair on his forehead, "what's the room number?"

Minutes later I rap on the door of number sixteen and wait. Silence. I try to look through the curtains, but they're drawn tight against spying eyes. I hunch low and check under the door. The door is about a half inch shorter than it should be. No light shines through. I knock again, wait. No answer.

Walking around the building, long weeds and empty cans connect with my boots every so often. I count the numbers backward and look in the rear window. This, I guess, must be the bathroom. There's no sound of running water, no light coming from the small square. Most of the rooms appear empty, though the neighbor in number seventeen is taking a shower. I walk back to the front of the motel and retrace my steps to the car, slide in behind the wheel. Who knows how long she'll be gone?

I lean back in my seat, the headrest wearing a familiar groove fitted to my skull. There is a dull hum of traffic on the interstate and images play behind my eyelids. I'm so tired. I didn't realize just how much until my eyelids get heavier and heavier ...

My eyes jerk open to the sound of a door slamming. I see a narrow band of light under the door of number sixteen and breathe a sigh of relief. The sooner I can get Patty talking, the sooner I can get the information I need and head home.

Hustling toward the door, I pat my jacket, making

sure that the can of pepper spray is in the pocket. It's doubtful I will need it, but still, better safe than sorry, right?

There is music playing from behind the door, seventies rock. The curtain moves as someone brushes past, and my heart does a somersault. I press myself close to the doorframe, glad that the porch light isn't on.

I kick myself for snoozing instead of remaining focused. If Patty is volatile, there could be ugliness. If she is surprised enough, though, maybe I can weasel my way into the room.

I knock twice, in what I hope is a friendly, non-threatening manner.

"Patty?" I call out. The music continues blasting. I knock more loudly and raise my voice. "Hey, Patty?"

This time there is a flutter at the window, the curtain pulls back momentarily and her face, white and topped with teased bangs, peers out. Then the face is gone and the deadbolt is being thrown. When the door opens, it's my mouth that's hanging open in surprise.

CHAPTER TWENTY-SEVEN

"Yeah. What do you want?"

Patty stands before me at least half a head shorter than my five foot four inch frame. But it's not her height that's surprised me. Braces run up each of her legs which bow inward, and her arms are supported on two metallic canes with rubber tips. She's clearly disabled. Why did I not see this in the photos? Why did no one mention it to me? I think back to my conversation with Jill. My own lies indicated that I knew Patty well, that we were old friends. Or at least, that we'd met face-to-face.

"What do you want?" Patty repeats. Her voice is agitated, and she glares up at me. Her poufy bangs and armful of neon jelly bracelets scream 80s, but the music in the background is more fit for a 70s nightclub.

"I, uh, sorry. My name is Tayt Waters. I'm from Franklin County, too, and I ..."

"You're coming by my room two hours away to tell me this?"

Her voice, previously annoyed, is bordering on rage-filled impatience.

"Uh, no. I ..."

The door starts closing in my face. I stick my foot

in at the last minute to which she responds with a loud, "Hey!"

"Sorry," I say, regaining what's left of my wits. "My name is Tayt Waters."

"You said that already, what are you a freaking parrot? 'Tayt Waters, Tayt Waters. Tayt wanna cracker?'" Her voice is high pitched and sing-song-y, and she snorts at her own joke. I grit my teeth. My senses are suddenly coming back. And now I'm feeling a bit pissy.

"You are Patty Commo, correct?" I say, my hand pressed flat and hard against the thin door. It feels slightly sticky, and I don't really relish the thought of flattening Patty against the carpet. Who knows what lives in there?

"Maybe I am," she says, chin jutting forward. The Kinks are raising their voices in a fevered pitch about Lola, and I push harder on the door. The effort of trying to balance herself on the canes and push against the door simultaneously is too much for Patty, and her body begins to slide sideways. I lurch through the space, grabbing her left arm before she falls.

Now it's my turn for a surprise. Her right arm shoots out of the cane and into my temple. Stars wobble before my eyes. For a scrawny woman, she has a mean hook. She pulls her arm back to have another try, but this time I'm ready. I grab her fist mid-flight and twist her arm behind her back. Hard. She yells, then whimpers.

"Hey! Let go, you're hurting me."

I loosen my grip but don't let go entirely. Who knows what's coming next? A head butt to the nose?

Fingernails scraping across my cheeks?

"Patty, I'm not here to hurt you. I was hired by your grandmother to find you." She continues to complain about her arm, but my eye is still throbbing hard, leaving little room left for pity.

I walk her backwards to the nearest bed, kicking the door closed behind us. She curses and complains some more. I push her onto the bed where she lays propped against the pillows, her feet akimbo near the night table. I go to the bathroom and get a drink of cold water from a surprisingly pristine glass with a little paper cover.

"Look, Patty," I say, drawing up a chair and sitting backward in it. I got off to a rough start and am determined to be business-like and efficient. "I've got a car out there," I wave to the door. "And if you'd like a ride home, I'd be happy to provide it. Your grandmother is worried sick; she's called the police." *Tiny lie.*

Patty's chin, which was jutting out, lowers when she hears about her grandmother.

"But first, you're going to tell me what Miller Stevens is into. And why you left town so fast."

Her head is hanging low now, and I worry that she's crying. Anger I can deal with, but tears are another matter. Then I think of her cat, rage in my chest covers any sympathy.

When Patty looks up her face isn't sad but furious, defiant.

"What is it to you? It's a free country! I'm calling the cops." Her left hand lurches toward the phone on the bedside table, and I panic, brain scrambling for ammunition.

"I'm sure they'd love to talk to you. You'll to be

fined for animal cruelty if nothing else." I wave at the phone. "Sure, give them a call."

Pause.

"What do you mean?" Her voice wavers slightly.

"I suspect it was Miller Stevens, but I can't prove it. Your trailer has been trashed and your cat ..." I'm walking on a limb here, hoping it doesn't break.

This is the last straw. Patty's face crumples, and this time tears, real tears and a lot of them, run down her face.

"What about Mr. Fluffy?"

Sob, sob.

"Is, is he," *gulp*, "dead?"

I nod.

She puts a hand over her mouth, the sobs coming louder in between her words.

"I didn't have any time, you know? Someone had been following me; I thought it was Miller or one of his goons. I just ran around as fast as I could, grabbing clothes and stuff. I kept trying to find Mr. Fluffy, but he was out hunting." She pauses to take a shaky breath.

"He loves hunting this time of the year; he'll be gone for most of the day sometimes. I called and called, but he must have been too far away to hear. What did Miller do to him?"

"Someone was at your trailer after you left," I say. "It was a wreck, clothes and stuff strewn everywhere. And Mr. Fluffy, well ..." how to say this tactfully. "He didn't make it."

The sobs turn to wails, and I turn awkwardly, pat her shoulder a few times. I'm not good at this comforting stuff, though, so I hand her a box of tissues and watch lines of light pass by the closed window curtains as traffic merges off the interstate ramp.

"Those bastards. I knew they were following me; I knew they'd come after me. That's why I left. I had to get out of town, get away from them. I tried to find ... and now he's ..." Her voice breaks off again into crying.

Many long moments later Patty has quieted enough to ask for a drink of water for herself. I go back into the bathroom, filling the other little glass and bringing it to her. She gulps it down in two swigs, and I ask if she wants more.

Nod.

I refill and return it.

"Why don't you let me bring you home?" I say. "You can tell me about everything that happened, about Miller and the sex trafficking and why he was following you ..."

She is shaking her head violently.

"I can't go back there. They've been in my house. They must have found," her voice halts awkwardly, stumbling over words, "what they were looking for."

I debate internally for a minute: give her the flash drive or keep quiet?

Digging in my pocket, I extract the small black rectangle.

"Is this what they were looking for? It wasn't in a very good hiding spot; I can't believe they didn't find it."

Patty smiles a slow, tremulous smile and reaches for the drive.

"Once you give me some information, it's all yours."

She frowns, her shiny silver eye shadow creasing between the folds of skin around her eyes.

"Fine. But can you take me to Burger King? I'm starving."

The interstate after eight o'clock is quiet. An occasional big rig passes and once in a while another car or SUV. There is no Burger King in Bellows Falls; the nearest one is about a half-hour drive away in Claremont. It's been a long day, and I'm looking forward to a bath and bed. Even if I was heading home right now, it would be nearly eleven before I get there. Rolling my shoulders, I glance at the passenger seat. Patty is full of noises of all sorts.

She sighs, heavily and frequently, complains that she's too hot, then, when I turn the heat down and crack the window, that she's freezing. She makes little noises indicating her displeasure while I scan radio channels. She's thirsty and has to use the bathroom. It's worse than traveling with a cranky two-year-old. I try to tune her out, but it's nearly impossible in such small quarters.

"Tell me about working for Miller," I say. She remains silent except for another couple of disgruntled grunts as she wiggles around in the seat, trying to get comfortable. I glance at her again. Her face is splotchy, and I feel badly now for using the cat as bait.

"I hate him." Her voice is low and angry.

"When did you find out about the sex trafficking thing?"

Between sniffles she starts. "He wasn't a bad boss as bosses go. I've had some real doozies, but Miller was sort of hands-off, let me set up the office the way I wanted, let me run with projects. He'd basically tell me what he wanted for an end result and set me loose. I liked that. Works with my personality.

"Anyway, there were, of course, downsides to working at a garage. You get treated like a dancing monkey for one thing, being the only woman in the joint. I can take the bathroom humor—I grew up with four brothers—but honestly some days I just wanted to knock heads together."

Patty interrupts herself to blow her nose. The sound is so loud I nearly veer off the road.

"It wasn't until I'd been there a while that I noticed something fishy going on with the accounting. Miller takes care of his own accounts, never had a professional on staff or a firm hired that I know of. He's good at it, so I thought it was weird when all these discrepancies started showing up. Money was being moved from one account to another, and new accounts at different banks were popping up left and right. At first I didn't pay much attention. Accounting isn't my strong suit and wasn't part of my job description, other than making sure that the money in the checking account was enough to cover that month's bills. But when the fourth new bank account opened in less than a month, I asked him about it.

"There were other things, too. The business was doing well, and I know his family has money. But once I started digging a little I found major money, in some of these accounts, most of it recently wired in by outside sources. That was weird, but before I could get more involved, things at the office changed."

"Changed how?" I ask, sipping my own coffee,

which is lukewarm.

I glance at Patty when there's no response. She's not exactly blushing but looks uncomfortable.

"Ah. I get it."

"It's never a good idea to sleep with the boss," Patty says, "but in this case, it was a really, really bad idea. I thought it was more than just sex, though, you know? I thought that he ..."

Her voice drifts off, and at the same instant my cell rings.

Crappy-crap.

I juggle the coffee and the phone until I get the cup into the holder. The cell's screen says *withheld* and I consider letting it go to voicemail, then change my mind.

My *hello* is answered by a disjointed sounding mechanical voice.

"You don't know what you're playing at. You should forget about this whole situation. Or you can choose to keep playing this game and be very, very sorry."

I pull onto the shoulder, cup my hand over my other ear and try to listen for background noises.

"I don't know what you're talking about." A slight tremor in my voice betrays me. "Maybe you've got the wrong number."

A low, disjointed chuckle from the other end. I picture one of those voice manipulating devices, like the scary guy in the white mask from the teen chill and thrill movies. I press my hand harder against my free ear, listen harder. Patty stirs in her seat, and I will her not to talk, not to ask any questions.

"Stop sticking your nose where it doesn't belong."

CHAPTER TWENTY-EIGHT

"And if I don't?" It's hard to breath. I hope that the caller can't tell.

Pause.

A low, mournful train whistle sounds in the distance on the other end, then the garbled voice speaks again.

"If you don't, then you and daddy are going to wish you'd never moved here. But your mother, now, she might come in handy. Pretty lady, isn't she?"

A throb starts over my left eye. I start to form another question, but there is only dead air. I stare at the phone for a few seconds then try the shortcut of keys that tracks incoming calls from hidden phone numbers. A longshot, but I still feel a pit in my stomach when I see "option not valid" on the last call that came through.

Slamming my hands against the steering wheel in frustration makes Patty jump in her seat.

"Geesh, what's going on?" I glance in her direction. Her poufy bangs have begun to collapse. I sigh and lean my head back, take a couple of deep breaths.

"Nothing. Just a bad day at the office."

Patty is quiet for once, and I check the side mirror then pull back onto the interstate.

Is Mama really in danger? We set up a security system when she first moved in, but half the time she forgets to set it. The other half she leaves doors and windows unlocked. I chew a hangnail, and Patty asks if she can change the radio station as the one we were listening to has morphed into static. I nod absently.

Pulling my cell back out, I punch in Ezra's number. I explain the situation, ask if he'd be willing to go and check on my mother. "Just make up a story about being in town, and then check that all the windows and doors are locked and that the security system is set when you leave. I have to …" I glance at Patty. I still don't trust her further than I could throw her. "I have to be somewhere else tonight."

"Sure, no problem." Ezra's voice is a welcome reassurance. "I actually was planning to be in the area later this evening picking up vestments and a few extra song books at another parish in town. I can stop over and check on your mother. Is there anything else you need?"

A hug. A protector. A big, loaded Uzi.

"No, thanks. I'm fine. Thank you so much for doing this, Ez. I appreciate it."

We hang up after I promise to call him in the morning and let him know how things are.

Patty and I are quiet the rest of the way to the fast food joint where she places an order for a Whopper with extra cheese, large fries and large diet Coke. I get a small packet of fries and a chocolate shake. We eat on our way back to the motel. Patty continues her story.

In addition to the strange accounts with excess funds popping up, she'd overheard Miller talking to people in New York City once and another time to someone in Montreal. He spoke of transferring goods, of picking up merchandise, but there were other words mixed in that made it clear that he was talking about people, not physical merchandise.

"Why didn't you go to the police?" I ask when she pauses to slurp at her soda.

She shrugs, looks out the window.

"Why doesn't any woman turn in the bad guy she's sleeping with? She thinks he loves her. Wants to believe he loves her and that he's going to change. Or that maybe she misunderstood something."

It's my turn to sigh. We don't talk much after that, the blackness of the highway soon becoming sprinkled with lights from the next exit. We arrive back at the motel and Patty prepares to get out of the car. She's sent a handwritten note for her grandmother, that she's visiting her cousins in Massachusetts and will be back soon.

"Will you?" I ask. She hands me the scrap of paper, and I give her the flash drive. "Be back soon?"

She shrugs, her fingers caressing the flash drive.

"I don't know. I guess so. I'll have to tell the police what happened, what's going on, right?" She looks at me for confirmation.

I nod.

"It's the best way to make sure that Miller gets prosecuted."

She sighs, gets out of the car, making two attempts before her canes hit the pavement simultaneously and she rights herself.

"I'll think about it. Thanks for dinner," she says. She looks somewhat older than she did just a couple of short hours ago.

The next morning I'm up with the birds. Literally. Despite getting to bed only hours ago, I'm replacing a piece of the roof that came loose in a recent storm. The *rat-a-tat-a-tat* of the metal piece smacking the rest of the roof has been like a slow dripping faucet, only louder and more annoying. My body might be tired, but my mind is dancing through possibilities like a polka aficionado.

Judy is on her way over, an early morning meeting. We talked, briefly, last night on my way home: she apologized again for having to reschedule yesterday's coffee. But with the news I've gotten from Patty, nothing in the world can possibly anger me.

Except ... is that the stupid cow again? A loud rustling and crunching in the underbrush comes from the farthest point of the driveway, but it's too dark to see. I look in that direction, hoping the beam of my headlamp will help, but the light isn't meant for long distances. I give a final couple of whacks with the hammer to the roof, put the extra nails and tools into my utility belt and climb down.

Carrying the extension ladder back to the shed, I hear the *crunch, crunch, crunch* of heavy feet headed my way. One would expect a cow to be louder than that, but perhaps Daisy or Buttercup or whatever her stupid name is has been taking bovine etiquette lessons.

"Go home, Daisy, or you're going to end up in my freezer. You've already finished off my flower garden anyway."

No response. No more footsteps. My heartbeat, fast

from the heavy load of the ladder, drowns out other sounds momentarily. I prop it horizontally on the ground near the shed and turn, wishing I had my high powered spotlight. I keep one on the back deck. It's captured everything from deer to bear in its rays in the early morning. The small beam of my headlamp outlines nearby shrubs and the raised garden beds near the deck. I walk in that direction.

I'm nearly to the deck when a gloved hand clamps over my mouth, another twisting my arm up sharply behind my back. I cry out at the shooting pain racing through my shoulder, but the pressure doesn't ease.

"You've got one hard head, Tatum. I told you to stay out of business that doesn't concern you." The voice is gravel-hard, breath warming my cheek. "You'll get a lot more than this if I come back here. Understand?" I nod mutely against the hand, my breath ragged.

I hate myself for being helpless. The pain in my arm has increased (who even knew that was possible?) and radiates from shoulder blade to wrist. Another hard jerk on it causes a fissure of sparklers to dance before my eyes. A tear wanders from my left eye, and I close them both to stop any more.

The same hand shoves me, hard, throwing me off balance and into the shrubs around the deck. My head knocks into one of the wooden posts but not hard enough to do serious damage. I lay still for a minute, listening to the sound of retreating footsteps over my ragged breathing. Then I scuttle toward the rear door holding my aching arm protectively with the other and click on the powerful spotlight. Feet run down the driveway and crash through the undergrowth near the road. I point in that direction but see nothing except the sway of still moving branches.

I curse, open the back door and grab for my gun, shoving it into my waistband as I run, following the invisible path through the undergrowth where I saw movement. The area is well lit by the spotlight at first, but even its strong beam can't cut through all the low branches and tangles of bramble. Blackberry bushes yank on my clothes, catch my hair, and I yell in frustration as I yank both free. I slip down a small ditch and up onto the dirt road in time to see the fading tail lights of a dark pickup truck. Too far away to make out a plate number or even the color or model. I curse again, stomp my foot on the road.

I run back to the trailer, this time on the road, and grab keys from the dish near the door, then hustle to my car and rev the engine. Reversing madly out of the driveway, gravel spews from the rear tires as the car lurches onto the road and down over the hill where the tail lights disappeared. I block out the logical voice in my brain telling me that this chase is futile, that the truck has a three minute advantage, not to mention a much higher horsepower engine. Careening around a corner, the car slips on loose gravel, and the steering wheel lurches under my hands. I crank the wheel left, then right, overcorrecting. A loud snap is followed by an even louder bang, and the car's right tire snags a low tree stump. The car whines in response, gives a shudder and stops moving.

I yell at the top of my lungs, hand banging the steering wheel as more expletives pour out of me, one with each hit to the wheel. The anger is raw and hot in my gut, searing my chest.

I scream, one pure, rage-filled, deafening screech. Then I lay my head back against the familiar headrest and suck in big gulps of air, wishing I were somewhere else. Anywhere else.

You're a real "security expert," all right. Why don't you just give this up and go back to cleaning houses for a living? At least you were halfway competent at that. My critical voice has the worst timing.

I extract myself from the car, still holding my sore arm gingerly, and walk around the front to survey the damages. The car's right wheel well is slightly crumpled, and worse, the tire on that side is jutting from the frame at a strange angle—like someone with a compound fracture—bone protruding. I sit on the hood, head in hand.

CHAPTER TWENTY-NINE

And that is how Judy finds me twenty minutes later.
I'd forgotten all about our early-morning meeting.

"What in the world happened here?" Her idling
vintage Saab putters and sputters. Light is just coming
up over the mountains in the east, and the sky is turning
all shades of melon: cantaloupe, watermelon, honeydew.

I sigh, climb off the car. My toes and fingers are
numb from the cold and I'm shivering.

"Long story. Can I climb in?"

She nods, takes another look at the crumpled front
end. I open the door and settle myself in the passenger
seat, not bothering with a seatbelt. Issues of *Bicycling*
and *Marathon* magazines litter the floor near my feet,
and I try to avoid mashing them with my boots.

"How long have you been sitting out there? You're
shivering." Judy glances at me, her hazel eyes bright.
You can almost see the wheels turning behind those
eyes, always moving, always imagining, popping with
never-ending ideas.

I fill her in, knowing it will earn me a lecture.

"You need to file a report," she says, pulling out her
cell. "Call it in."

"No way. This is personal, and I'm not going to

give him the pleasure of seeing that his antics made me sweat. I'll handle this myself."

Judy sighs.

"This isn't a game, Tayt. What if he comes back? You didn't do such a great job defending yourself this time."

"Gee, thanks." I sigh, my cheeks puffing out. "He caught me off-guard, that's all. I know how to protect myself."

Judy puts the phone in the console between us. Sighs.

"I know you do." Her voice is quieter. "So what happened this morning?"

I look out the window. What did happen? Why didn't I react the way that I'd been trained? The first rule of self-defense is being aware.

"I guess I let my guard down. It's hard to be thinking "awareness" twenty-four seven, you know? I was distracted, my mind working through some other stuff."

Judy nods once.

"Your dad."

Not a question. She knows me.

"I should have realized when I heard the footsteps that they were human, not bovine."

"You get a lot of miscellaneous cow visitors?" Judy smirks at me as we pull into the driveway. She lets the engine idle and studies my face, her smile fading.

"I know you're going through some really bad stuff right now with your family. But we're going to catch the creep who's responsible, I promise. And in the meantime, you've got to take care of yourself, Tayt.

You'll be no good to your family if you're—"

"Dead."

"Well. I was going to say incapacitated, but dead wouldn't be good either." She smiles again. "Let me do my job, and you concentrate on your job, and we'll get there together, OK?"

I nod.

"OK." She reiterates. "I've got some good news, by the way. You got coffee on?"

We settle at the scarred table fifteen minutes later, steaming mugs between us. Judy has a notebook before her, as always, it's legal sized and yellow. She has two pens as well, the same type that line her office closet by the box load. Did I mention she is ADHD and anal retentive both? When she gets supplies, she gets enough for a decade, because to Judy, boring details like keeping the office stocked is way down on the list of interesting things to do in life.

Her leg jiggles beneath the table. "So, what I've found is pretty interesting. Remember I said I was going to do some digging on your pal Miller Stevens?"

I nod, take a sip of coffee. If I don't hear that name again for twenty years, it will be too soon.

"It turns out that Mr. Stevens did a little jail time back in the day. College days to be specific. I found some old drug charges—trafficking and using—as well as two alleged date rapes. Both girls ended up backing out of the cases, saying that they were drunk and couldn't remember what happened, *frat-party-and-wild-nights-har-har*. But when I made contact, one was willing to talk. She talked a lot as a matter of fact."

"Would she be willing to on the stand?"

Judy smiles, sips her coffee.

"Yes."

A wave of relief washes over me. Finally someone is in our corner. It's not just us pointing fingers at Stevens' camp and them pointing fingers back at us. And if Sam pulls through this afternoon ...

"I've got more."

"I love you, Judy."

She grins.

"I know. I get that a lot. Here's what I found."

We spend the next hour talking through the details she's uncovered. The wave of relief I mentioned? Increase its power by ten. There are still a lot of unknowns, a lot of variables that could shift things pretty quickly from *Team Judy & Tayt* to *Team Stevens*, but now there is a little glowing ball of hope in my chest.

It feels good.

And then I get a phone call that turns my world sideways.

The call comes just after eleven o'clock. Judy left two hours ago, and I've been doing piddly little home-maker crap: laundry, sweeping, dusting, taking out the trash and recycling. I do them once a week, tops, and spend much of the time being thankful that I wasn't born in the fifties. Cleaning for money is much different than cleaning for free.

My cell phone gives a muted chirp, and I find it buried in my jacket under the coat hooks. *Caller unknown.*

"Hello?"

Breath, heavy and deep.

Silence.

Pause.

"Hello?" I try again, my voice sounding irritated. Which makes sense because I *am* irritated.

Silence.

I'm about to disconnect when the voice on the other end speaks.

"Tayt?" Another breath, then a gasp. The voice is female and she's crying.

"Yes, I'm here." I wait a minute for the voice to speak again.

"Tayt, I need help. I run away—"

"Alinah?"

Choking sob.

"Yes."

"Are you OK? Are you hurt? Where are you?" I'm already stuffing my good arm into a jacket, pressing the phone hard against my ear. Grabbing for keys.

"Gas station. . . Main Street." *Gasp, sob.* "Please, you come?"

I get the location details as I'm jogging to the car.

"Do you want to stay on the phone until I get there?"

"No. But you hurry?"

"I will."

It's not until after I hang up that I realize my car won't be driveable, at least not for a while. I wish for the eightieth time that Winston had a phone. I walk to the end of my driveway, about to make the mile-long trek to his house, when I hear the grinding of a large tractor nearby. Winston, atop a mammoth red tractor, is toting my car back toward his house. I wave my arms.

"How did you know about this?" I motion to the car behind us, craning my neck upwards to see him in the tall seat.

"Heard something earlier, came down to check it out. You should have come over straight away; I would've been here sooner."

"I know you would have. Thanks for doing this; I really appreciate it. Is it something you can fix?"

Winston scratches his head, a John Deere cap bobbing up and down repeatedly.

"Think so. Bent that wheel good, but I seen worse." I chew my lip.

"I've got another problem. I have a sort of emergency and seeing as I can't drive that," I wave my hand over my shoulder, "I was wondering if—"

"You can take the Ford if you want. It'll need some gas, though."

I jump up on the step of the tractor and squeeze his forearm in an awkward hug.

"Thanks. I owe you one."

Winston shrugs off my hand, but I see a smile pulling the corner of his lips up.

"Just what neighbors do."

The gas station is brick and looks like thousands of other gas stations in thousands of other small towns across the country. Six pumps on three islands, a trash can in between with a pocket built in for a window washing brush. Signs in the windows boast sale prices on beer and gallons of milk. A lone man, head bent, stands near the store's entrance scratching lottery tickets

and cursing under his breath as I approach the door.
I'm about to walk inside when I see Alinah.

CHAPTER THIRTY

Small and hunched, with her knees drawn up to her chest and a thin jacket drawn over top, she's sitting on a picnic table near the rear parking area.

I jog over, then slow my approach when getting close. I don't want to scare her.

She glances up just as I enter her peripheral vision. Her eyes are red with tears, but her face is as beautiful as ever. Strands of hair loosened from the braid behind her head tangle over her nose. She's shivering.

"Come on," I say, pulling her arm gently. "The car is warm. I'll go get you some coffee or tea if you want."

She shakes her head.

"Thank you. No. Thank you for coming."

"No problem."

I help her into the car, grab an extra blanket from the back seat and place it over her. She snuggles in and leans her head back. Then she sighs the deepest, longest sigh I've ever heard. She's exhausted, I realize. How many hours, days, did she plan her escape?

Putting twenty dollars of gas in the Ford's tank, I snag some snack foods: plastic packages of crackers with peanut butter, nuts in cellophane wrappers, a couple of candy bars and two bottles of juice. I ask for a bag and take my haul to the car.

Alinah smiles wearily when I unlock the door and get in. I want to plead with her to explain, ask her a trillion questions and drive her anywhere in the country she wants to go. I want, I realize suddenly, to protect her. Just like my kid brother. I haven't felt that instinct inside for a long time. I glance at the passenger seat before pulling out into traffic. Deep breathing and motionless, Alinah has already escaped into the world of sleep.

Following back roads, I bite my fingernails. Where am I going to take her? My place is ruled out. After the incident this morning, I feel less than safe. Winston's? I doubt that even a S.W.A.T team could get through his security system unscathed. But it's still a little close for comfort. I need to hide Alinah somewhere private and out of the way and completely unrelated to my home or office. I toy with the idea of my father's place. Jack certainly isn't using it, but there may be stray cops or detectives around even now.

I stop for a coffee at McDonald's then worry that someone in the drive thru might recognize my passenger and be a friend of Miller's. Scooting out of line, tires chirping, I glance to the cars behind and in front.

Gnawing another nail, I head north on the interstate. Brilliant gold and orange trees flank the still-green grass, making it look like we're moving through an oil painting. The sky is so blue it appears dyed, the clouds fluffy and white and perfect. The idea comes finally as most great ideas do: like a bolt of lightning shot directly from overhead.

The camp.

Twenty-five minutes later I'm shaking Alinah's

shoulder gently. She jerks upright, eyes wild, hair tangled over her face.

"It's OK. It's just me. Tayt," I say, voice low. "We're at a house in the country. The owners live out of state and won't be back until next summer. You'll be safe here." Her eyes widen as she takes in the beautiful garden, the curling walkways circling bed after bed of dying flowers and the small camp tucked neatly between hundred year old trees.

Alinah puts fingers to her mouth.

"It very pretty." She smiles and I do, too.

I get Alinah settled in the house, show her how to turn on the small electric fireplace and find her a couple of ratty but clean towels that I left behind the other day. She'd told me how much she'd like a hot bath. I promise to stop by in an hour with more food and some of my extra clothes, blankets and sheets for the bed in the guest room and some paper and a pen that she asks for. Through our conversation Alinah's eyes remain sad, often brimming over with tears. Is she thinking about Sarjana? Feeling irrational guilt that she's here and finally free while her friend's body has been shipped back home?

"Tayt?" She calls quietly as I walk toward the door. I pause, hand on handle and look over my shoulder.

"You're not going to thank me again, are you?" I smile, trying to lighten the mood. Her eyes are bright with wobbly tears. She shakes her head.

"I dream of doing this for many years. But I never could do ... alone. You know?"

I nod then clear my throat.

"I'm glad that I can help you, Alinah," I say finally. She nods once, twice. "You'll be fine here, and I'll be back soon with some supplies."

I turn to go. Then, "Oh, I almost forgot. Take this." I pull an extra can of mace free from my pocket and give her a thirty-second lesson on how to use it. I also give her the small bag from the gas station, and she clutches it to her chest like a life vest. Then, finally, a smile breaks out on her face. Wide and warm and whole.

I smile back, then pull the door closed behind me, check it twice to make sure it's locked and walk back to my borrowed car.

I call Ezra's connection, Seth, at the immigration office in Burlington, but a recorded voice tells me he isn't able to answer my call. I debate leaving another message while the voice drones on and in the end leave a simple one: that I'm a friend of Ezra's and that I have a question about immigration, a pressing matter, and am hoping he can help. I leave all three of my numbers and finish it off with the obligatory, "Hope to hear from you soon," code for, "Don't be a slacker. I needed this information yesterday."

The phone call is placed en route, back to the camp where Alinah is already falling asleep on the couch. I move the supplies in quietly and leave a note by the pay as you go cell phone that has my office number, home number and 9-1-1 programmed into it in case of emergency. I also leave a map of St. Albans Bay, in case she goes exploring. I doubt she will, but personally I would freak out if I were trapped somewhere without knowing what was around me. I think of all she's been through and what it must be like to be trapped and held against your will, used for sex ... and then I have to stop myself from thinking further because blood is pounding in my ears and temples and I feel that slow, hot crawl of rage in my gut. I take a few deep breaths, make sure that both doors and all the windows are locked, then head to the car.

I have a date.

Sam Wells may be an irresponsible, pot-smoking loser, but he is punctual. We meet in the rear lot of my office building, and I hustle him upstairs before anyone can see him. He's on edge, hooking a finger around the blinds and peering across the street then shuffling his dirty sneakers in another corner of the room. Agitated. Can't sit still.

"You're not getting cold feet, are you?" I ask, holding up an empty coffee cup with raised eyebrows.

He shakes his head.

"No. And no coffee either."

I shrug, make a cup for myself and then sit at the desk while it brews.

"So?" I make a show of widening my hands, in an, *I'm-here-and-willing-to-listen-to-you-spill-your-guts* motion.

He rubs the back of his neck with a rough-looking hand, then sighs and plops down on one of the chairs facing me.

"So, here's what I know about Miller and your father. That night, Sunday, I went with Miller up street to Doug's." He nods toward the white Victorian across the street. "He said he needed help with something. We picked up one of the girls, I don't know her name, the small one with short hair and a friend of Doug's, a guy named John. John followed us up in his truck. Said he didn't know the way and told Miller he'd better go slow. Cops are out more at night lately, trying to catch DUIs I guess.

"It was late, real late. After midnight at least. We drove up to a place in the country, some renovated barn or something. I didn't realize then that it was your dad's place."

My heart is hammering in my chest.

"Miller said John would take care of the girl; he needed to talk to someone and set things up for the next day. I didn't know what he was talkin' about and I was dead tired. I just sat in the truck and waited. She didn't speak very much English, the girl, but she looked scared. John brought her to the door. They went in. Miller met someone outside, old guy with scraggly hair. Looked like a bum. They talked for a minute, then Miller handed him an envelope, and the old guy left on foot.

"Miller was in the barn with John maybe fifteen or twenty minutes. Told me to stay outside, let them know if I saw anyone. Who's going to be out that late at night in the middle of the country? I saw one car pass the whole time, probably some half-asleep jerk just getting off the late shift. Anyway, Miller came back out, like I said, about fifteen, twenty minutes later."

"Just Miller?" I interrupt.

Sam nods.

"What happened to John and the girl?"

He shrugs. "I asked if we were waiting for them, figured she was doing a job, but Miller said no and we just left. He had his own ride, so I didn't think much of it."

There's a small hiss from the coffee pot; other than that the room is silent. I lean back in my chair. I feel alternately elated and sickened by his story.

"And you can testify to all of this? We can make it anonymous, so that there's no way that Miller will know it's you."

Sam snorts.

"How dumb do you think I am? Of course he'll know it's me. There's no one else that has this kind of first-hand information. Look, I'm not worried about Miller. Me and the wife have been talking about moving out of that dump on the hill for years. I figure, now's our chance.

"We can start fresh somewhere. Maybe go out West—I've always wanted to see Montana." He crosses his right leg over his left at the ankle, legs spread before him. If he was twitchy before, telling his story has eased his anxiety. His whole body appears relaxed, from face to ratty sneakers. I want to snort. As if he'll be allowed to leave the state. Accessory to murder, obstruction of justice ...

"Look, Sam, can you tell me everything you just did one more time while I record it?"

"Why?"

I shrug, rest my arms on the top of my desk.

"Might save you a trip back to Vermont if this goes to trial." *A lie. Because it will go to trial.*

"I guess." Sam draws his legs back under his chair. "But first I want something."

My hand stops its motion of fishing in the right

upper drawer for my digital recorder. What now? Money? Pot? His bottle of gin that I gave my mother?

"And what would that be?" My voice sounds like my least-favorite teacher in high school.

"I want my cap back."

I smile, pull open another drawer and extract the disgusting ball cap still in the plastic grocery bag, tossing it to Sam. He catches it neatly from the air, pulls it free of the bag, and in a single fluid motion, slaps it onto his head.

"Better?" I ask.

He nods, and I press the record button, sliding the small unit as close to the edge of the desk as possible.

"This is Tatum Waters, speaking with Sam Wells of Bakersfield, Vermont. Sam, do I have your permission to record this conversation?"

"Yes."

"Today's date is ..."

CHAPTER THIRTY-ONE

The rest of the day passes in a blur. Two calls from my mother, which I let go to voicemail, (yes, I'm a horrible daughter), informing me of Sophie's recent promotion ("Isn't that wonderful? Finally some good news for our family!") and more requests to get my father to change his plea from innocent to guilty.

I keep an eye on the white house across the road throughout the afternoon. Sam didn't go back there after we met, saying that instead he was going to spend time at The Trap and then catch an early movie. I assume that avoiding Miller, at this point, is his goal. He can't go home in case police are checking the premises. He doesn't have other family in the area. I don't know where he's planning on sleeping tonight and didn't ask. As long as he doesn't leave town, I couldn't care less where he crashes.

Two men enter the white house at different times; both stay approximately a half hour. I have the camera set up in the window on a tripod, and even though I lost the beautiful, high-powered lens in the lake, I snap a few pics of the potential perps using an older, scratched telephoto lens. I think of Judy and mentally ask forgiveness. But when this goes to court, and she's in need of evidence, she'll appreciate my efforts.

Still, the thought of Judy and her reminders that my job now should be focusing on my caseload cause a quick press of guilt in my chest. Dinner is leftover takeout from the small fridge in the office which I eat while taking care of some long-overdue paperwork. I leave a little after nine o'clock.

The lights at the gas station on the corner of Lake Road and Maquam Shore Road are blazing bright when I pass by. I drive slowly, partially to keep an eye behind me via the rearview mirror and be sure no one is following, partially because I'm exhausted, and my eyes are getting heavy.

Turning the heater off, I crank open the driver's side window. Cold air floods the car and instantly I sit a bit higher in my seat. My plan is to crash at the camp tonight, hopefully without terrifying Alinah in the process.

I debate calling and leaving yet another message on Seth's voicemail but don't want to piss him off. I'll try again first thing in the morning and just keep calling without leaving messages. Hopefully the office phone doesn't have caller ID, or he might think I'm a stalker.

The cottage is dark when I arrive, and I'm able to get in and settled without waking Alinah. My brain is whirling in a caffeine-induced way, and as soon as my head hits the pillow I'm wide awake. Tossing and turning for more than an hour doesn't bring sleep.

I bundle up in an old sweatshirt, a pair of jeans and some heavy woolen socks and take up residence on a rocker on the back deck, a pen and loose leaf notebook on my lap. I start out drawing circles, making connections between people and places they've been. Some circles are big and have lots of lines going to and from them, Miller Stevens' obviously with the most. After a half hour the page is nearly covered, every circle has at least one connection. Every circle except one: Jack's. How does he tie into this? Why frame him?

The stars are bright and the moon is full, making shadows in corners of the porch but lighting my pad of paper without a need for flashlight or lantern. Wind moves through those leaves still on branches, the sound like an old-fashioned pen and ink set, scratchy and dry. Other than that, there is no sound.

Then my cell lets out a digital burp, destroying the moment. A text message. I reach for it and see Judy's name, push a button and read: "Have info on Simon George. Call me in the a.m."

I punch in her cell number, and she answers on the first ring.

"Did I wake you up?" Her voice is as bright as early morning sun. Does the woman ever rest?

"No. I can't sleep. What did you find out about Mr. George?"

"Ah, wait till you hear this. I got in touch with my army buddy, and he did a little research for me. Actually, it turned out to be a lot of research because everything in the military is ten times more complicated than it needs to be."

I picture Judy whipping the generals and corporals into shape and smile. "Anyway, it turns out that Simon George—that's his real name by the way, not a very creative fellow—told your father the real story. He was a mechanic, worked on tanks, *blah-blah-blah*, and was honorably discharged years ago. After that, though, he suffered some sort of mental breakdown and spent a little time in the VA hospital and then just disappeared."

"Became a drifter?"

"I guess so. I also found some connections locally—places he's stayed, people he's talked to, friends he's made. Mostly other street people. These people aren't ones to talk openly; they like their privacy. Learned the hard way that sharing too much information can be dangerous. But I found a woman, Claire, who opened up to me. Anyway, long story short, I've located Simon, and he's in custody down in the Rutland area. I'm going to see him tomorrow, have a little chat."

I nearly squeal in happiness. "Judy, you really are amazing. That's awesome news!"

She blows off the compliment, tells me to get some sleep and that she'll follow up with me tomorrow after she's spoken to our friend Simon.

I lean back in the rocker and look at the stars, my breathing slowing. The creak of the old chair is comforting. The last thing I hear before drifting off to sleep is the pad of paper sliding onto the deck.

I wake up hours later with the sun poking me rudely in the face and my neck twisted at an odd angle. For a second, I can't remember where I am and then I do. My stomach growls loudly. My tongue feels pasted to the roof of my mouth, and it takes a few minutes to extract various body parts from the chair and stretch them out. Sleeping in the old rocker wasn't the best thing for my arm, it reminds me, snippily, as I head into the camp.

It's nearly eight o'clock my cell phone display says. Tiptoeing into the other room I find Alinah still asleep. Should I wake her up and make breakfast for both of us? I decide against it. After everything she's been through, sleep is more necessary than food. I wash up quickly in the small bathroom and brush my teeth, run a comb through damp hair.

Double checking that the back and front doors are locked, I trot out to my car. I've left Alinah a note telling her that I'll call her later this morning. Hopefully by then I will have some good news from Seth to report.

I grab breakfast at a small coffee shop on Main Street, the dry, warm smell of freshly ground beans nearly making me swoon. A cup of dark roast paired with some sort of delicious pastry are inhaled as I make my way to the office. Traffic is heavy this time of morning, and I wait impatiently for yet another person in the crosswalk to make their way across the street.

Finally, I make the turn onto Lake Street. The big white house across the street is dead silent as I flick on lights in the office and settle at my desk, turning on the old computer and licking pastry bits from my fingers. I burned my tongue on the first sip of coffee—that's what happens when you try to suck it down like lemonade—and it stings now with every subsequent sip.

The first phone call I place is to the jail, asking when I can stop over to talk with Jack. The officer I talk to reminds me that visiting hours are between nine and ten and again in the afternoon between four and five. I ask to be put on the list. Thanking him without sounding the least bit sarcastic (well done!), I hang up.

A minute later my phone rings. It's Seth from the

immigration office. I picture him, an older guy with a beard maybe, leaning back in his office swivel chair. We go through the polite formalities and make a bit of small talk about Ezra, our common denominator. Finally, I get to the point.

"I have a hypothetical question for you," I say. "Let's just say that someone was in the country illegally but without consent. Say kidnapped or forced into labor here in the U.S., what would happen to him or her if they were discovered by authorities? And would there be anyone to help them get back home?"

Seth clears his throat.

"The process can be somewhat long and drawn out, I'm sorry to say. I've known cases where the illegal may sit in jail for weeks, sometimes months, before they're deported. They usually have no paperwork, which is problem number one. It takes time to file everything, fill in all the documents, dot the i's and cross the t's. Well, that's problem number two actually. Problem number one is the fact that they've entered the country illegally."

I sigh.

"Hypothetically speaking though," Seth says, his voice lowering to nearly a whisper, "the situation is somewhat different. I owe Ezra a favor—about ten of them to be honest. So if there was a man or woman who was in need of some speedy assistance in fleeing the country, and it was for a good reason, I'd likely be able to help him. Or her."

I perk up in my chair and launch into a quick recap of Alinah's story, leaving out the part about her friend's death and my father's potential involvement in it. No need to smear mud on what might otherwise be a golden opportunity. Seth makes a lot of "uh-huh" type noises throughout my story, and I picture him nodding along, sipping out of a big mug as he listens. Forget immigration. I think this guy missed his calling as a therapist. Finally, I stop, and there's a moment of silence on the other end.

"Listen, Tayt, I think I can help you—I mean your friend—your hypothetical friend, that is. I'll need a day or two to set some things up and then there will be the matter of the travel arrangements. She would need a plane ticket and I'm guessing a ride to the airport. And she would also want to make contact with someone back home. Find out if there is any family or a friend who can help her once she gets there. Otherwise, she'll likely find herself in as bad a place there as she was here.

"You might also try contacting House of Hope." I madly scribble details onto a scrap of paper. "They run homes for former trafficking victims in many countries around the world. You could see if there's a place for your friend."

I nod. "Right. I'll take care of it. Thank you."

"Other logistic," Seth continues, "she'll need some cash to help her get started. Travel documents I can take care of, should be able to get that pushed through quickly. Government pensions aren't so great anymore, but one of the perks of working here for thirty-plus years is the ability to call in favors now and then."

Seth clears his throat. "I've got two daughters of my own. I can't imagine ..." his voice cuts out momentarily, and I fill in the gap.

"Thank you again," I say, scribbling notes about airplane tickets and checking my bank account. "This is a complete cliché, but I can't tell you how much this will help."

"So many of these cases don't have happy endings," Seth says. "I'd be happy to know that I might be part of one that does."

CHAPTER THIRTY-TWO

I make a flurry of phone calls before going to visit Jack. First Ezra, thanking him again for checking on my mother last night and asking if he might loan me a couple of hundred dollars. When he finds out what it's for, he insists that I take the money without the worry of repayment.

I consider calling C.J. and asking for help transporting Alinah to the airport, maybe hitting him up for a little more cash to help get her started, but my pride stands in the way. Stupid as it may be, I recognize this is a mountain I can't climb today and move on to the next number on the list: Sam's wife. It's been days since I last made contact with her, and my belly twists with guilt. The phone rings five times, then six, and I'm about to hang up when a tiny voice answers.

"... lo?"

"Hello. This is Tayt Waters. I'm trying to reach your mom." Loud baby wails erupt in the background.

"Mom?" The little voice asks me.

"Yes, is your mother there?"

There is a bump, then a thump, and then the crying gets louder. Much, much louder. I picture one of the kids I saw the other day dragging the phone, literally, to his mother.

"Hello? Are you still there?" I say after several long seconds of listening to the baby screech.

Finally, a woman's voice answers the phone. Or at least she tries to, but is nearly drowned out by the wailing infant. Her voice is exhausted, and I make yet another mental note to never spawn a child.

"Mrs. Wells, this is Tayt Waters."

The baby quiets a little, and I hear a gentle *thump-thump-thump* and picture the poor woman patting the squirming back of Poltergeist Baby.

"Sam?" Her voice breaks and then she's crying, quietly and tiredly. I wait impatiently for her to speak again.

"Have you found him?"

"Found him? You haven't heard from him?"

"No. Not since ..." her voice is drowned out by some more, louder thumps, and then one of the older kids screaming about his brother taking his toy. Another child begins screaming, and I picture much hair pulling and flailing fists. She shushes them, and the baby finally settles down and I wonder for the thousandth time how any of us survived the human race without our mothers eating us alive.

"Sorry. They're a little wound up today."

I make a sympathetic noise and she continues. "I haven't heard from Sam in more than two days. The last time I talked to him, he was ranting about Montana and leaving this state behind us and starting over and getting a van from someone he knows to move. He was supposed to call me back last night, but I haven't heard from him. He always calls when he says he will." She stresses "always."

"I'm sure he's fine," I say. "I talked to him, and he's actually helping out with an investigation. He told me he was going to lay low, trying not to draw unwanted attention to himself or your family."

"When did you talk to him?" Her voice is hope-filled.

"Yesterday afternoon."

"Something's happened to him. I know it." The hope has run out of her voice and is replaced by the wobble of fear. "He told me he'd call last night, and he always does. He might be an ass sometimes, might make stupid mistakes, but if he says he'll do something, he does it."

I think about his punctuality and the fact that he followed through for me when he said he would. A shiver runs down my back and goose bumps pop out on my arms.

"Let me check around town, OK? Don't panic yet."

She gives a wry chuckle. "Too late," she says, as yet another child starts whimpering near the phone.

Jack is already at the visitors' table when I arrive. He looks cleaner than last time I saw him and not quite as gray.

"The guard said you were coming to see me and that I could come down and wait for you." His voice is quiet and sounds like it does when he first wakes up, rusty. I guess he doesn't talk to a lot of people here.

For a minute I want to laugh. How crazy and upside down our lives have become! My father in jail for murder. My mother hanging on by a thread. My best friend helping me transport a sex trafficking victim out of the country. What happened to worries about bills and car insurance and normal everyday annoyances like bad drivers and nighttime TV?

"I don't have a lot of time this morning but wanted to see how you were."

"And?"

"And what?" I spread my hands out innocently.

Jack wears the same expression I've known since childhood. The one that says, "I know what you're up to, so you can save me the show." I swallow once, twice and then say, "OK. I have some good news, but first I want you to tell me about anyone and everyone in your entire life that might possibly have it out for you."

"You mean besides your mother?"

I roll my eyes, drop back in my seat. My parents bring out the thirteen-year-old in me.

"Give me a break. Are we really going to get into this again?"

My father looks down at his hands, rubs them together. They make a dry, scratching sound. Then he looks back at me.

"No, we're not. I'm sorry. It was a joke. Sort of." He smiles halfheartedly.

"I don't have time for jokes, Jack."

He nods. "Sorry." He stares off into space for a second. "I don't know, Tatum. Not really, no one I can think of. And I have been thinking about this, believe me. Judy asked me the same thing, so did the police detective. I'd love to jump in with some brilliant idea, to remember someone who hates my guts, but," he spreads his hands wide, "I can't."

I try to hide my discouragement. What did I think? I'd jiggle his memory with this obvious question and the key person in the murder investigation would come popping from his lips? That'd be nice. That's how it works in the movies, but apparently, not in real life.

"Well, I have some good news. Judy learned that not only was the supposed eye-witness who saw your car fleeing the site of the murder bogus, but Simon George is in custody, down in Rutland. Judy is questioning him this morning. I don't know more than that, but it's a great start. She's going to be calling soon with more information, and then she or I will get in touch with you."

His eyes close for a moment, and then a smile, tired and wan, spreads over his face.

"That's good news. Thank you, Tayt." He opens his eyes and looks directly in mine. I want to look away, suddenly uncomfortable, but I hold the glance.

"You're welcome," I say, but the words sound stiff, like cardboard.

"I mean it. I know we aren't in a good place as father/daughter, but you've done a lot to help me, more than I deserve ..."

I suddenly think of Ezra's words at the restaurant, about forgiveness. I'm not ready for that. But I do lean across the table and pat one of Jack's hands. He looks at me, surprised, then grips my fingers and gives a strong squeeze.

I leave before he can thank me again. When I glance over my shoulder before the door shuts behind me, I see him paused in the hallway, hands in shackles, watching me go. Something like admiration perches on his face, and for some stupid reason this makes me want to cry.

Driving through the city, I make circles on side streets and slow down as I pass every alleyway. Sam Wells has to be here somewhere. I stop at the local library, the pharmacies and one grocery store downtown, then the gas stations and liquor store, showing his photo to everyone I meet. Many nod their heads in recognition but none have seen him recently. I try The Trap but the lone bouncer/barman doing early cleanup says he hasn't seen him for a couple of nights.

Where else might he be? He wouldn't be stupid enough to go back to Miller's place on the lake, would he? Unless he thought his missing presence would spark alarms. Maybe Sam thought it less suspicious to keep to normal routines, though that's not what he said when he was in my office. He was trying to avoid Miller, not get back into the circle.

Still, with few other leads to go on, I drive to the shore, past the dock at St. Albans Bay and around a rotary that spits me onto a farm-lined road with cows munching happily at dried up looking grass.

I try Alinah's cell phone, but there's no answer. Maybe she's taking a shower or sitting in the hammock outside. I leave a message, let her know that I'll be there around lunchtime and that I have some good news to share.

Miller Stevens' house is just as ostentatious as it was earlier in the week. I drive past, then pull into what looks like an unused driveway of a summer house and park. Walking back to the grove of trees across from his

house, I nestle myself in the brambles and leaves.
Without binoculars or the fishing hat and vest, I doubt
I'll make a very convincing bird-watcher today.

Nearly an hour later, there is finally movement in
the house. First a young blonde woman dressed in a
short, silky robe lets out the two hulking beast-dogs.
They run frantically around the yard peeing on
everything multiple times.

Ten minutes or so pass and then Miller strolls out,
muscled legs tanned in nylon basketball shorts and a pot
belly pressing against a t-shirt that looks a size or two
too small. He yells to the dogs, and they return to the
house then he continues on to his truck and climbs in. I
eye the house, then the truck. Which one?

I hustle back to the car and follow Miller's truck.
For once, he's actually traveling the speed limit. I hang
back, far enough that I don't think he'd be able to pick
out the make and model of my borrowed car.

Miller makes a sharp right onto a dirt road, and I
follow, slowing even further. The dust from his truck
will hopefully hide most of the cloud my own car is
kicking up. I don't know this road. It starts out flat and
straight but is soon winding through trees and up and
down small hills. I worry at one point that I will bounce
right out of the car; the potholes are so large. The road,
already narrow, gets even thinner; its width is reduced to
a single lane. I can't see Miller's truck anymore. I speed
up slightly over the rise of the next hill and then slam on
the brakes, holding in a scream.

The black truck is stopped length-wise across the
road, Miller leaning against it. Waiting for me.

CHAPTER THIRTY-THREE

I fumble in the bag next to me on the seat for my gun, but the bag is empty. Then I remember: I'd used the bag to transport clothes and food to the camp. I must have left the gun at the house.

Jamming the stick shift into reverse, the car lets out a groan. Miller starts walking quickly toward the passenger side, then breaks into a jog and finally a full on run. For a stocky guy, he's surprisingly fast. I push the gas pedal to the floor, and the car starts to zoom backward. I'm watching Miller and not my rearview mirror, however, and the zoom lands me in a small spread of saplings. The car's tires whir, and the engine whines as I crank the wheel and try to get the car's nose in the opposite direction.

I'm just about to clear the turn when Miller launches himself into the small interior of the car. I gasp in shock, and he grunts in response, then grabs onto the wheel and jerks it sideways. We wobble for a minute. The edge of the road is so close. My heart feels like it's going to explode in my chest as I look over the ravine on my side of the car.

"Are you crazy?" I scream.

He grunts again and then jerks the E-brake up. The

small Ford whines, and I hear a strange crunching sound come from under the hood.

"Get off me, Miller!" I flail at him with both arms, but he shrugs off my hits as though they were mosquitos. Finally, I come to my senses and retreat as far back into my corner of the car as possible then launch a right-hook to his face. It hits him squarely in the jaw, and his head snaps back. He looks at me, first in surprise, then rage.

He swears at me, grabbing a fistful of hair and slamming my face into the steering wheel. I try to turn to the side, so he won't break my nose but only make it part way. Fireworks explode in my eyes when my left cheek and the left side of my forehead and nose make contact. I feel blood in my mouth before more runs from my nostril. How much more would it hurt to bite through one's entire tongue instead of just the side? I try to hit him again, but the seat makes an awkward angle. He still has my hair in his meaty grip. I sink my fingernails into his forearm. This is rewarded with a yell but unfortunately, also another crash into the steering wheel.

Then his hands are around my throat, and he's whispering in my ear that he's going to make me pay, make me pay, make me pay … and then there is only darkness.

When I come to, the first thing I notice is that my head has grown three times its normal size. At least that's how it feels. It throbs—my face especially—like one of those old cartoons where the thumb that's smacked with a hammer pulses and glows red. The second thing I notice is that I'm in a semi-dark room. My hands are bound above my head, feet bound and stretched out to the corner bed post nearest me. I try moving my fingers, but blackness comes again before I can test them out.

When I wake up again I feel pain in every square inch of my body. I'm also incredibly thirsty. A gag has been put in my mouth, and the fabric is pasty. I try to call out, but the sound comes across as more of an *aahaa aaaahahhh* than a real word. Still, it is enough to draw attention. The door across the room opens, and Miller's form fills the space.

"Well, well. Hello, sunshine." He strolls across the room, grinning. I fantasize about leaping from the ropes and drop kicking him in the head, but instead, sit helplessly and stare at him.

"You know, this could have all been avoided if you hadn't been so nosy," Miller says, drawing closer. He crouches near me, and I can smell sweat and the lingering odor of pot. His hand trails up my leg, and I close my eyes in disgust. His fingers are calloused and cold and everything in my being screams at me to *do something do something do something*. But I can think of nothing to do.

"Ahhha ahhha ahh?" I try to form words around the gag. Miller chuckles, and his hand moves from my leg to my face. In one deft, ungentle move, he yanks the gag free.

"You're not going to yell or scream or do anything else, right?" He holds the gag, still tied, around my throat. "I'd hate to have to finish you off before we have our fun but ..." he sighs, lifts his shoulders as though to say *what will be will be*.

"No," I say, my throat dry and the words hoarse. "No screaming. Can I have some water? Please."

He chuckles again, and the sound raises the hair on the back of my neck. I realize suddenly where we are. This room is familiar to me. The camp. My heartbeat thunders loud in my ears, and I suddenly feel nauseous. Where is Alinah? I picture her in various bloody poses and close my eyes, trying to wash away the images.

"Not just yet," he says, smoothing back hair that's fallen out of my bun.

"I think me and you are going to have a little talk, then a little fun. Then maybe I'll see what I can do about a drink. How's that sound?"

Terrible. The worst thing I've ever heard of.

"OK," I say. "But can I please get out of these ropes? I'm not going anywhere. I mean, we're pretty much in the middle of nowhere here. There's really nowhere I *can* go." My voice is scratchy and rough, like I've been a pack-a-day smoker for the past twenty years.

Miller thinks about this for a moment, surveys my legs and arms and finally nods.

"Fine. You're going to be needing all those parts soon anyway." He grins, and I nearly vomit. "But if you even think of running or doing anything else stupid, so help me ..."

I nod. And nearly blackout.

He leaves the room, and I notice a handgun, small, snub-nosed, tucked into his waistband. When he comes back a moment later, Alinah is trailing behind him. A huge breath I didn't even realize I'd been holding whooshes out of my chest.

Thank you, God. Thank you, God. Thank you, God.

She's alive and all in one piece.

Her face looks different, though, and she doesn't make eye contact with me as Miller instructs her to cut my bonds free. Her hands are gentle when she wipes at the dried blood on my wrists, trying to smooth it away. Miller watches her.

"That's enough. She's fine. Give me the knife." He waits for her to obediently turn over the blade. "Now go to the other room and stay there."

She turns, mechanical almost, and I finally realize what looks different about her. Her face is like a mask, expressionless, emotionless. Shock? Or maybe acceptance that her short freedom has ended.

Miller points to the bed.

"Have a seat." He continues standing by the door. I want to call out to Alinah to grab a weapon—a chair, a lamp, anything—and smash Miller's head. Instead, I perch at the edge of the bed, every muscle and tissue and bone in my body aching. The throbbing in my face and head is slightly lessened, maybe because I now feel all this pain in other parts of my body.

"You think you're a lot smarter than you are, you know that?" Miller says. "Did you really think that we didn't know you took her? That you could hide her right under my nose? I have friends everywhere, Tayt. Everywhere." Miller glances away from me toward the window and crosses to it.

I react before my body can protest. Lunging off the bed, I grab at his waistband. He turns, fist already coming toward my head. I jerk my face away, and he misses, the punch throwing him off balance.

"Alinah!" I scream. He's reaching for me again, but

I have the gun, try to fire and realize the safety must be on. Instead, I whip it toward his face, cracking him solidly across the nose. He lets out a scream and blood begins to gush.

Alinah moves toward me, holding something in her hands, then she shoves past me and crashes a small footstool down onto Miller's head. A split of skin opens and more blood pulses out. He curses and claws toward Alinah, his right hand grabbing her throat. With one quick move, he forces her body upward, pinning her to the wall. Blood continues to flow down his face and his snarling lips.

I'm moving in slow motion, my body and brain not working in synch. I look for the gun's safety and turn it off, then press the barrel against the back of his neck.

"Put her down, now, or I'm going to splatter your meager brains all over this wall," my voice sounds strange in my own ears, the s's lisping because of my swollen lips.

He holds her there another second, and my finger starts to pull the trigger. Then he whirls, throwing her limp body across the bed like a rag doll, and spins toward me. My finger slips from the trigger, then re-grips. I pull. The shot misses his ear by an inch, and the bullet lodges itself into the wall. I can't hear anything except a pounding roar from the gun's retort in my head. I see Miller's open mouth and imagine he's yelling but hear nothing.

Then his hand is on the gun, along with mine, and our fingers are slipping, and then we're wrestling and kicking and there are arms and legs twisting and turning. We fall to our knees. Miller has a good eighty pounds or more on me, but the fight isn't in the size of the person, I remember my sensei telling me.

It feels like we've been grappling for hours, but it's been only seconds. Then he knocks me to the floor, and we're still scrabbling for the gun. I want to scream but have no air. Alinah rises from the bed, holding her throat, and I can finally hear something over the roar in my head.

"No, please," she says, moving toward Miller. "Please no hurt her." Miller's face is ugly with rage, and he turns toward her, adjusting his weight from my torso. Breath comes flooding back into my lungs, and I jam a knee into Miller's groin as hard as I can. He yells and turns to backhand me, but I roll to my side. His fist glances off the floor, and he gives another yell, this one filled with rage.

I scramble to my feet and then hear the gun go off again, this time missing Alinah by inches. A hole in the wall near her head scatters plaster which clings to her hair and clothes. She screams and starts to cry.

Miller aims again, his arm wobbling with fatigue. I jump without thinking and feel a burst of white-hot pain in my right shoulder. It's so intense I think I'm going to collapse. My hand immediately goes to the wound. I feel warm wetness. I want to pull my hand away, inspect the damage, but there is no time.

Alinah is crouched on the floor in a tight ball, arms over her head. Miller looks from me to her and smiles. I stumble toward him, blood dripping. Launching myself forward, I smash the top of my head into his nose. It breaks immediately, I can tell by the crunching sound.

He howls and collapses to his knees, meaty hands

going reflexively to his face. I waver on legs that feel ready to give out, bend down and pick up the gun. It's warm in my hand. I don't think, just point and shoot. I see a hole in the wall, and blood splattering.

And then I see nothing but blackness.

CHAPTER THIRTY-FOUR

There is white everywhere, as though I'm trapped in a cloud. My body isn't flying, though, it is weighted and heavy and every single part of me hurts. I try to open my eyes. The lids, though, are so heavy and I'm so tired ...

Words are being spoken. No, not words. A prayer.

"Though we travel through the valley of the shadow of death, we will fear no evil." I open my eyes and see dimly, a priest, sitting nearby, a halo of light around his head. "You prepare a beautiful banquet for us, in the presence of all our enemies." I turn my head slightly which causes a burning feeling down my neck.

"Tayt?" The priest leans close.

Not quite a priest.

"Am I dead?" My words are garbled, blurred together like a watercolor painting.

Ezra chuckles, moves close to the bed and gently lifts my hand, which is caught in a snarl of wires and tubes.

"No, not dead. You're too ornery to die and too smart to let Miller have the last word." His smile fades. "God, I'm so glad you're OK. We thought we were going to lose you."

I try to smile but imagine the result is frightening. "Alin. . .ah?"

Ezra smiles wider. "She's fine. She's right next door."

I try to say, "that's good," but it comes out more like *thasssgoo*.

He sets my hand gently back onto the mattress. "I'm going to go tell the others that you're awake. We're only allowed in one at a time, but your mother and Judy and C.J. are out in the hall waiting." I try to nod, but it hurts too much, so I just close my eyes again and wait.

Tears slip out of the corners of my eyes, and I want to brush them away, but it's too much effort. I slip back under the blanket of blackness before the next visitor makes it into my room.

The last thing I see before my eyes close is Miller's ugly face on the television screen across the room from my bed with the words "late breaking news" running across the bottom of the screen.

EPILOGUE

In the end it was Alinah who saved me. She'd created a weird tourniquet/sling out of the bed sheet for my shoulder, then called 9-1-1. Thankfully, I'd left that map for Alinah, so she had an address to give them. I'd remembered to program the emergency 9-1-1 number in Alinah's phone before I'd given it to her, too, not knowing it would save me. So, take *that*, stupid critical voice.

My mother and Ezra met the ambulance at the hospital, Mama a mess of tears and wringing hands, Ezra calm and collected by comparison, I would imagine. They'd taken up residence outside the ICU and gotten in touch with Judy. C.J. was one of the officers responding, and he'd flown up to the hospital. He had been there ever since.

I wasn't sure which part of the story Ezra told surprised me most: that he and C.J. had been able to sit for hours alongside each other without a single argument erupting or that my mother hadn't had to be given horse-sized amounts of tranquilizers.

In the weeks that followed, more surprises awaited me, some good and some not. If I were to make a list in my notebook, here's what it would look like.

The Good List: Jack released after learning that a former business associate, Lawrence Stevens, a great-uncle of Miller Stevens, was behind the murder and incrimination. Apparently Lawrence was not only royally irritated that my father used to whip him in their bi-weekly golf games but that an investment in my father's company had tanked.

The Stevens family isn't big on people letting them down, and Lawrence was convinced that my father's involvement in the financial loss was not only purposeful but also planned. He swears that my father led him on, feeding him bits and pieces of information about the software company's financial portfolio and getting him to bite. When that particular branch of the company closed, the investors lost their shirts.

Jack had no recollection of these conversations, other than as friendly golf-game chatter. Lawrence's hospitalization for attempted suicide and the subsequent findings at his apartment detailing his involvement were enough for his attorney to decide to keep him off the witness stand at the trial. There are more questions around Sarjana's death which are still without answers though. Jack's memory of that time is completely blank and Simon knows only that he was paid, by Miller, to give Jack a drink laced with a heavy sedative, Rohypnol. The popular drug of date rapists, it's scarily easy to obtain.

Another positive was Alinah's safe return to Malaysia. She is part of a women's recovery group home, and the last time we talked on the phone she was working as a waitress, participating in therapy sessions during her free time. She plans to go to school for a degree in nursing.

The sex trafficking ring went underground, and this would be on the bad list except that Judy is determined to get to the bottom of it. I doubt very much that the perps stand a chance. The case really affected her: She's become an advocate for the same anti-sex trafficking organization that her niece is involved with and is working to raise money for it through a triathlon she's putting together in the Waterbury area.

The Not Good List: Sam Wells was found dead in Lake Champlain near the boat dock in St. Albans Bay. Official results haven't been released yet, but authorities are suspicious. I saw a short news clip of the story, and the sight of his widow and four little kids clinging to her was hard to take. I'm ashamed of myself, but I have yet to call her. I will, though, as soon as I can.

Number two on the bad list: the fact that the owners of the cottage are taking me to court. They are suing for damages which my insurance company says that they are not responsible for. So much for being a Good Samaritan.

I'm at home now after a month of hospitalization and rehab, and Winston checks in on me twice a day. Between him, my mother, Ezra, C.J. and Judy, I'm about at my wit's end with conversation.

I know they were all worried and that they mean well, but it's hard to have any peace and quiet, even this far out in the country, with all the impromptu visits and phone calls. I want to hang a sign outside that says, "I'm still fine. I'll call you when I'm dead."

My body isn't healing as quickly as I'd like it to, and it's hard not to worry about things like bills and caseload while you're holed up in your house and being treated like an invalid. A nurse comes once a day to help me with my bath (a job that C.J. volunteered for in front of my mother, who nearly hyperventilated in horror) and to make sure I'm taking my medicine correctly. Honestly, I was shot in the shoulder not the head, so I'm not sure why there are all these worries about my memory or mental abilities. Ezra says that people have always been worried about my mental abilities, that I shouldn't let this bother me. I would smack him, but it requires too much effort.

Mostly I just sit around and watch bad daytime television, read gardening magazines and dream of the day when I can get back into my office for full days of work. And get back to the gym. The physician who is treating me said that my stellar conditioning played a huge role in my survival. So there, exercise naysayers. All those hours really are good for something.

Soon I'm going to go into the office and grab some files and some phone lists, just to stay on top of things. I've had to hire someone on temporarily to man Repo Renew for me. Cindy's a hard worker, and she has a lot of energy, like Judy. If she's interested, maybe I'll consider selling her the business. It would be nice to have just two jobs again.

But right now I've got a lot on my mind. C.J. told me about another missing person, and even though I'm not yet up to the task, I've asked him to keep me in the loop. My mother protests and Ezra rolls his eyes; both want me to focus on "just getting better." But C.J. gets it. I can't be better without my work. It's becoming part of me, part of who I am.

And if I'm not there to help the next person, who will be?

ABOUT THE AUTHOR

What do you get when you cross a performer and an introvert? A novelist, of course! J.P. Choquette knew she wanted to be in the performing arts early, acting as all manner of animals and trees in grade school productions. Shyness, however, can be a real downer for those on stage, so she turned her flair for the dramatic to pen and paper, creating "books" held together with staples and glue.

Writing professionally since 2007, J.P. has published three books and is currently at work on a fourth. She lives in Vermont where she enjoys drinking hot beverages, taking long walks and making junk art … just not all at the same time.

Find out more about the author by visiting her website, www.jpchoquette.com

30778139R00167

Made in the USA
Middletown, DE
06 April 2016